Get a Feel for English !

喚醒你的英文語感！

Get a Feel for English !

喚醒你的英文語感！

老闆要你學英文
職場句型篇

總編審：王復國
作者：吉田研作、荒井貴和、武藤克彦
「完全改訂版　起きてから寝るまで英語表現700 オフィス編」

●利用本書的句型結構，在職場中培養更好的傳達力及表現力

　　本系列書籍的基本概念為：以<u>一個人就能進行英語會話</u>的想法為基礎，將工作場合中所能想到的、感覺到的一切都化為言語，用自言自語的方式來練習。

1）用英語描述自己的動作（I text my colleague.）

2）將自身所處之情境化為英語（This room is full of computers.）

3）用英語說明自己當時的感覺（I feel so tired after answering so many e-mails.）

4）將當時所想、所感覺到的一切都化為英語（I'm not sure if this job is really what I wanted to do.）

　　本系列的基本概念，就是將上述各種狀況以自言自語的方式說出，成為表達自我之工具。一般人都會以為自己的經驗就只專屬於自己，但是其實每個人的經驗與其他人的經驗常具某些共通之處，很容易引起共鳴。因此，本書所蒐集的各種表達句型可以適用於各種不同人物。相信很多人都曾有過「對對對，就是這樣。」、「我也是。」、「原來不是只有我這麼想。」這類的經驗。的確，不論世界怎麼變化，只要同為人類，基本的生活經驗不致相差太遠。

　　本書之學習法乃由法國學者弗朗索瓦　古茵（Francois Gouin）於 19 世紀所開發之教學方法發展而來，透過以英語表達自身行為、情

緒、想法等方式，達成提升英語傳達力及表現力之目的。期盼本書句型能有效幫助各位讀者提高自身的英語表達能力。

上智大學外語學院英語系教授　吉田研作

Contents
目 錄

本書結構與使用方法
How to Use This Book

本書整體結構與使用方法

■將一般上班族從上班到下班為止的一日場景分成 10 章。

■各章又再分成「單字篇」、「身體動作」、「自言自語」、「Skit（對話）」、「Quick Check（測驗）」等部分。

■讀者可從第 1 章開始依序閱讀，也可從自己較有興趣、與自身狀況類似的部分開始閱讀。

■只要利用本書所收錄與辦公室內外活動相關之英語句型，反覆進行「自言自語的練習」，你就能有效提升自己的職場英語口說能力了。

各章結構與使用方法 ─────────────

〔單字篇〕

■在此會將各場景中各種周遭事物的單字和對應的插圖一同搭配呈現。而這些單字幾乎都會出現在後續「身體動作」和「自言自語」部分的例句或說明中。

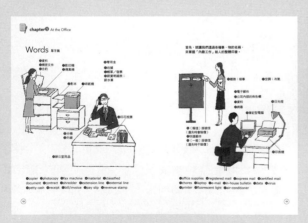

※首先，請試著將插圖內的中文翻譯成英文，解答就在下方。透過此單字篇，讀者便能對該章產生一個概略的印象。這就等於是在全力學習各種英語表達方式前，先做個暖身運動。

〔身體動作篇〕

■列出各場景中常進行之行為、動作的英語敘述，也就是，將外在行動轉化為語言敘述。這類句子通常看似簡單，但是要用英語講時，卻常說不出口。請一一聽取，並不斷反覆練習說出這些你每天都會進行的動作，直到徹底記住為止。

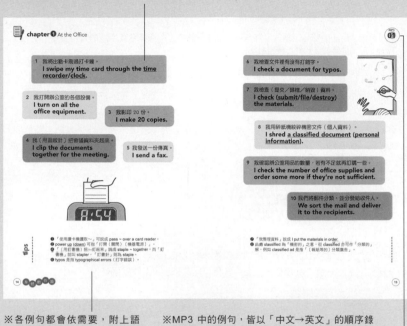

chapter ❶ At the Office　　MP3 01

1 我將出勤卡刷過打卡鐘。
I swipe my time card through the time recorder/clock.

2 我打開辦公室的各個設備。
I turn on all the office equipment.

3 我影印 20 份。
I make 20 copies.

4 我（用釘書針）把會議資料夾起來。
I clip the documents together for the meeting.

5 我發送一份傳真。
I send a fax.

6 我檢查文件裡有沒有打錯字。
I check a document for typos.

7 我檢查（提交／歸檔／銷毀）資料。
I check (submit/file/destroy) the materials.

8 我用碎紙機絞碎機密文件（個人資料）。
I shred a classified document (personal information).

9 我確認辦公室用品的數量，若有不足就再訂購一些。
I check the number of office supplies and order some more if they're not sufficient.

10 我們將郵件分類，並分發給收件人。
We sort the mail and deliver it to the recipients.

tips
● 「使用讀卡機讀取」可說成 pass ~ over a card reader。
● power up (down) 可指「打開（關閉）（機器電源）」。
● 「（用釘書機）摺～釘起來」叫做 staple ~ together，而「釘書機」就叫 stapler，「釘書針」則為 staple。
● typos 是指 typographical errors（打字錯誤）。

● 「我整理資料」說成 I put the materials in order。
● 原意 classified 為「機密的」之意，但 classified 亦可作「分類的」解，例如 classified ad 是指「（報紙等的）分類廣告」。

14　　15

※各例句都會依需要，附上語意、句型結構等能幫助你了解其表達方式的說明。

※MP3 中的例句，皆以「中文→英文」的順序錄製。請先將全書讀過一遍，再練習聽完中文後就立即說出英文來。

怎樣才能將句型記得更牢？

請利用 MP3 中所收錄的例句或對話來進行「跟讀練習」。所謂的「跟讀練習」就是一邊聽，一邊將所聽到的句子立即覆誦出來。越是將發音、節奏、語調模仿得維妙維肖，效果就越理想。一開始讀者也許很難跟上 MP3 的速度，但是只要不斷反覆練習，就一定能說得流利。而屆時，不論是單字還是句型，都將成為你的一部分，徹底烙印在你的腦海中。

〔自言自語篇〕

■本篇處理的是心裡或腦中的「內在」世界，也就是，列出大腦或心裡所想事情的各種表達方式。而這類「將以自己為中心的內在世界言語化」，意即，「自言自語」的表達方式，其實比千篇一律的會話句型要豐富、有趣得多。

※雖然「自言自語」部分也納入了許多可應用在會話中、能表達自身情緒的實用說法，不過一開始還是以自言自語的方式練習較好。

※MP3 中的例句皆以「中文→英文」的順序錄製。請先將全書讀過一遍，再練習聽完中文後就立即說出英文來。

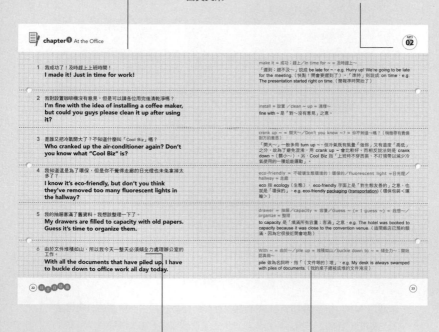

MP3 02

1 我成功了！及時趕上上班時間！
   I made it! Just in time for work!

   make it = 成功；趕上／in time for ~ = 及時趕上~
   「遲到」趕不及~」說成 be late for ~ 或「遲到」。e.g. Hurry up! We're going to be late for the meeting.（快點！開會要遲到了）。「準時」則說成 on time。e.g. The presentation started right on time.（簡報準時開始了）

2 我對設置咖啡機沒有意見，但是可以請各位用完後清乾淨嗎？
   I'm fine with the idea of installing a coffee maker, but could you guys please clean it up after using it?

   install = 設置／clean ~ up = 清理~
   fine with = 是「對~沒有意見」之意。

3 是誰又把冷氣開大了？不知道什麼叫「Cool Biz」嗎？
   Who cranked up the air-conditioner again? Don't you know what "Cool Biz" is?

   crank up ~ = 開大~／Don't you know ~ ? = 你不知道~嗎？（機能帶有責備到方的意思）
   「開大~」一般多用 turn up ~，但冷氣若有風量「強弱」，又有速度「高低」之分，故為了避免混淆，用 crank up ~ 會比較好。而相反說法則是 crank down ~（關小~）。另，Cool Biz 指「上班時不穿西裝，不打領帶以減少冷氣使用的一種節能運動」。

4 我知道這是為了環保，但是你不覺得走廊的日光燈也未免拿掉太多了？
   I know it's eco-friendly, but don't you think they've removed too many fluorescent lights in the hallway?

   eco-friendly = 不破壞生態環境的；環保的／fluorescent light = 日光燈／hallway = 走廊
   eco 指 ecology（生態），eco-friendly 字面上是「對生態友善的」之意，也就是用「環保的」。e.g. eco-friendly packaging (transportation)（環保包裝＜運輸＞）

5 我的抽屜塞滿了舊資料。我想該整理一下了。
   My drawers are filled to capacity with old papers. Guess it's time to organize them.

   drawer = 抽屜／capacity = 容量／Guess ~ (= I guess ~) = 我想~／organize = 整理
   to capacity 是「填滿所有容量；客滿」之意。e.g. The hotel was booked to capacity because it was close to the convention venue.（這間飯店已預約的額滿。因為它很接近開會地點）

6 由於文件堆積如山，所以我今天一整天必須傾全力處理辦公室的工作。
   With all the documents that have piled up, I have to buckle down to office work all day today.

   With ~ = 由於~／pile up ~ = 堆積如山／buckle down to ~ = 傾全力~；開始認真做~
   pile 做為名詞時，指「（文件等的）堆」。e.g. My desk is always swamped with piles of documents.（我的桌子總被成堆的文件淹沒）

※標題的英文與中文，彼此不見得是直譯的關係。本書所列出的是最適合表達該感覺的道地英語。

※各例句都附有說明，能幫助讀者了解其表達方式，甚至進一步理解語意和句型結構，並學到更進階的單字及說法。

〔Skit 對話〕

■在此提供彙集了各章句型而成的會話形式，以協助讀者將已學到之表達方式應用於實際對話中。請將此部分視為活用所學句型之實踐單元，並把自己當成會話中之主角反覆練習。

※曾出現在「身體動作」、「自言自語」等部份的表達方式，會以褐色標出。

〔Quick Check 小測驗〕

這裡的題目以出現於各章中但並未出現於 Skit 部分的句型為主。請依據中文的意思，來完成對應的英文句子。若碰到不懂的句型，就隨時翻回對應頁面去複習。

〔本書的各種標記說明〕

在本書中，除了特別標註的部分外，都以美式英語之標記、發音為準。此外，各種標記符號的說明如下。

cf.	參考比較以下資訊
e.g.	以下為舉例
＿＿／＿＿	斜線前後有底線的部分可相互替換，意思仍不變
[ ]	可加上 [ ] 內的單字、片語
( )	可替換為 ( ) 中的單字、片語（但意思會改變）

9

MP3使用方法　Directions for the MP3

■以內文中的 MP3 標誌來確認音軌編號

聽 MP3 時，請先查看每個小單元開頭處所標記的 MP3 音軌編號，以便讓 MP3 播放機直接播放該部分。

■MP3 音軌標誌

 在每個小單元開頭處，此光碟圖示上所寫的數字，就是 MP3 中的對應音軌編號。

■收錄內容

身體動作篇
自言自語篇
Skit 對話篇

■收錄時間

約 107 分鐘

■收錄語言

中文＋英語
→所有句型都同時收錄了中文與英語版本。請先將所有句型都了解一遍，再反覆練習，直到一聽完中文，便能立即脫口說出英語為止。

■音軌表

Chapter	頁　碼	音　軌
chapter 1	012-041	**01–03**
chapter 2	044-071	**04–06**
chapter 3	074-097	**07–09**
chapter 4	100-121	**10–12**
chapter 5	124-153	**13–15**
chapter 6	156-177	**16–18**
chapter 7	180-207	**19–21**
chapter 8	210-227	**22–24**
chapter 9	230-257	**25–27**
chapter 10	260-281	**28–30**

辦公室內
At the Office

早上進公司，先打個卡，
然後接電話、處理文件、電腦作業、
收發信件…
在此將為您介紹普遍存在於各行各業之
內勤員工們共通的身體動作、行為及內
心想法。

Words 單字篇

❹資料
❺機密文件
❻合約

❶影印機
❸傳真機

❿零用金

⓫收據
⓬帳單／發票
⓭薪資明細表；
薪水單

❷影本　❼碎紙機

⓮印花稅票

❽分機
❾外線

⓯辦公室用品

❶copier　❷photocopy　❸fax machine　❹material　❺classified
document　❻contract　❼shredder　❽extension line　❾external line
❿petty cash　⓫receipt　⓬bill/invoice　⓭pay slip　⓮revenue stamp

首先，就讓我們透過各種事、物的名稱，
來掌握「內勤工作」給人的整體印象。

⑲雜務；瑣事　　　　　　㉗空調；冷氣

㉑電子郵件
㉒公司內部的佈告欄
㉓資料
㉔病毒

㉖日光燈

⑳筆記型電腦

⑯〔報值〕掛號信
（遺失時會賠償）
⑰快捷郵件
⑱〔一般〕掛號信
（遺失時不賠償）

㉕印表機

⑮office supplies　⑯registered mail　⑰express mail　⑱certified mail
⑲chores　⑳laptop　㉑e-mail　㉒in-house bulletin　㉓data　㉔virus
㉕printer　㉖fluorescent light　㉗air-conditioner

1 我將出勤卡刷過打卡鐘。
I swipe my time card through the <u>time recorder/clock</u>.

2 我打開辦公室的各個設備。
I turn on all the office equipment.

3 我影印 20 份。
I make 20 copies.

4 我〔用迴紋針〕把會議資料夾起來。
I clip the documents together for the meeting.

5 我發送一份傳真。
I send a fax.

tips

❶ 「使用讀卡機讀取～」可說成 pass ~ over a card reader。
❷ power <u>up (down)</u> 可指「打開（關閉）〔機器電源〕」。
❹ 「（用釘書機）把～釘起來」說成 staple ~ together。而「釘書機」就叫 stapler，「訂書針」則為 staple。
❻ typos 是指 typographical errors（打字錯誤）。

6 我檢查文件裡有沒有打錯字。
I check a document for typos.

7 我檢查（提交／歸檔／銷毀）資料。
I <u>check</u> (<u>submit/file/destroy</u>) the materials.

8 我用碎紙機絞碎機密文件（個人資料）。
I shred <u>a classified document</u> (<u>personal information</u>).

9 我確認辦公室用品的數量，若有不足就再訂購一些。
I check the number of office supplies and order some more if they're not sufficient.

10 我們將郵件分類，並分發給收件人。
We sort the mail and deliver it to the recipients.

❼ 「我整理資料」說成 I put the materials in order.
❽ 此處 classified 為「機密的」之意，但 classified 亦可作「分類的」解，例如 classified ad 是指「〔報紙等的〕分類廣告」。

11 我接電話。
I answer the phone.

12 我打內線電話給某人。
I call someone at his extension.

13 我〔幫某人〕轉達電話留言。
I pass on a message I took [for someone].

14 我將來電按保留要對方等候。
I put the call on hold.

15 我確認工作流程。
I make sure of the workflow.

⓫ 「拿起電話」說成 pick up the phone。
⓬ 「外線」是 external line，e.g. Please dial 0 first for an external number.（要打外線時請先撥 0）
⓭ leave a message 就是「留言」。
⓰ 「精簡化」說成 streamline，e.g. We'll streamline our

16 我檢討工作流程以排除不必要的工作。
I review the workflow to eliminate unnecessary jobs.

17 我們傳閱簽呈。
We circulate a petition.

18 我請我的主管簽核文件。
I have my boss sign the documents.

19 我在合約的兩端上蓋章（蓋騎縫章）。
I affix a seal over two edges of the contract.

20 我保持桌面整齊（乾淨）。
I keep my desk <u>organized</u> (<u>clean</u>).

operations.（我們會精簡我們的業務運作）
⑱「蓋公司章」就說成 put the official seal on a document。
⑲ seal 指「印章；印信」。個人使用的「圖章；私章」叫 name chop。
⑳「整理桌子」說成 I clear my desk.。

21 我記錄零用金的流向。
I keep track of the petty cash.

22 我發薪資明細表。
I issue a pay slip.

23 我報帳。
I claim my expenses.

24 我把訪客帶到會客室。
I show a guest to the drawing room.

25 我在大廳與訪客碰面。
I meet a guest in the lobby.

tips

㉑「記帳」説成 keep <u>books</u>/<u>accounts</u>。

㉓「我提交費用申請書」説成 I submit an application for my expenses.。

㉕「我將訪客送到門口」説成 I see the guest off at the entrance.。

㉗ budget proposal for the next fiscal year 就是「下一個會計年度的預算提案」。

26 我做企業計劃。
I make a business plan.

27 我做預算計畫。
I make a budget plan.

28 我計算總銷售額。
I work out/calculate total sales.

29 我宣布財務結算結果。
I announce the financial results.

30 我請總裁做最終的裁決。
I ask for a final decision from the president.

❷❽ 此例句也可改用 tally（清點；核算）這個字，說成 I tally total sales.。
❷❾ 「財務報表」說成 financial statements，而「會計期間」是 accounting period。
❸⓿ I submit something for the president's approval. 就是「我提交某物請總裁批准」。

password

31 我將電腦開機。
I start up my computer.

32 我掃描病毒。
I scan for viruses.

33 我檢查（送出）電子郵件。
I <u>check</u> (<u>send</u>) my mail.

34 我瀏覽公司內部的佈告欄。
I browse the in-house bulletins.

35 我設定密碼。
I set the password.

tips

❸❶ 「我重新啟動我的電腦」說成 I reboot my computer.。
❸❷ keep the virus-checking software up to date 就是「讓防毒軟體維持在最新版本」。
❸❸ 「回某人的信」說成 answer someone's mail，而「轉寄郵件」則說成 forward the e-mail。

36 我設定印表機。
I set up a printer.

37 我從內部網站下載文件。
I download documents from the intranet website.

38 我將文件轉成 PDF 檔。
I convert the document to a PDF.

39 我整理資料。
I sort the data.

40 我與負責的部門聯繫，通知他們我電腦出了問題。
I contact the department in charge about a problem on my computer.

❸ browse 就是「瀏覽網頁」的意思，但 browse 也可指「隨意翻閱」，例如，I browsed through some magazines.（我隨意翻閱了幾本雜誌。）

❸ set a printer to a high resolution 就是「將印表機設成高解析度」。

❸ sort 有「分類；區分」的意思，而「從資料庫中抽出資料」說成 extract the data from a database。

1 我成功了！及時趕上上班時間！
I made it! Just in time for work!

---

2 我對設置咖啡機沒有意見，但是可以請各位用完後清乾淨嗎？
I'm fine with the idea of installing a coffee maker, but could you guys please clean it up after using it?

---

3 是誰又把冷氣開大了？不知道什麼叫「Cool Biz」嗎？
Who cranked up the air-conditioner again? Don't you know what "Cool Biz" is?

---

4 我知道這是為了環保，但是你不覺得走廊的日光燈也未免拿掉太多了？
I know it's eco-friendly, but don't you think they've removed too many fluorescent lights in the hallway?

---

5 我的抽屜塞滿了舊資料。我想該整理一下了。
My drawers are filled to capacity with old papers. Guess it's time to organize them.

---

6 由於文件堆積如山，所以我今天一整天必須傾全力處理辦公室的工作。
With all the documents that have piled up, I have to buckle down to office work all day today.

make it = 成功；趕上／in time for ~ = 及時趕上~

「遲到；趕不及~」説成 be late for ~，e.g. Hurry up! We're going to be late for the meeting.（快點！開會要遲到了）。「準時」則説成 on time，e.g. The presentation started right on time.（簡報準時開始了）

---

install = 設置／clean ~ up = 清理~

fine with ~ 是「對~沒有意見」之意。

---

crank up ~ = 開大~／Don't you know ~? = 你不知道~嗎？（稍微帶有責備對方的意思）

「開大~」一般多用 turn up ~，但冷氣既有風量「強弱」又有溫度「高低」之分，故為了避免混淆，用 crank up ~ 會比較好。而相反説法則是 crank down ~（關小~）。另，Cool Biz 指「上班時不穿西裝、不打領帶以減少冷氣使用的一種節能運動」。

---

eco-friendly = 不破壞生態環境的；環保的／fluorescent light ＝日光燈／hallway = 走廊

eco 指 ecology（生態），eco-friendly 字面上是「對生態友善的」之意，也就是「環保的」，e.g. eco-friendly packaging (transportation)（環保包裝＜運輸＞）

---

drawer = 抽屜／capacity = 容量／Guess ~ (= I guess ~) = 我想~／organize = 整理

to capacity 是「填滿所有容量；客滿」之意，e.g. The hotel was booked to capacity because it was close to the convention venue.（這間飯店已預約額滿，因為它很接近開會地點）

With ~ = 由於~／pile up = 堆積如山／buckle down to ~ = 傾全力~；開始認真做~

pile 做為名詞時，指「〔文件等的〕堆」，e.g. My desk is always swamped with piles of documents.（我的桌子總被成堆的文件淹沒）

7　可以麻煩你影印 10 份第一季的財務報表嗎？
Will you make 10 copies of the financial statements for the first quarter?

8　他總是要我幫他做事。他不能偶爾自己影印一下嗎？
He's always asking me to do things for him. Can't he make a photocopy once in a while?

9　每次我用回收廢紙影印，影印機就會卡紙。
The copier gets jammed every time I use scrap paper.

10　影印機似乎出了點問題。我應該馬上叫維修人員過來。
Looks like something's wrong with the copier. I should ask maintenance to come right away.

11　我的傳真送不出去，因為出現傳輸錯誤。
My fax message couldn't be sent because of a transmission error.

12　最近我看不太清楚小字……該不會是老花眼了吧？
I'm having trouble reading small print these days...Are my eyes getting that old?

make copies of ~ = 影印～／financial statements = 財務報表／first quarter = 第一季

copy 可作動詞用，例如 copy onto A4 paper（影印在 A4 紙上）。

---

make a photocopy = 影印／once in a while = 偶爾

once in ~ 是「每～一次」之意，故 once in a while 就是「每隔一段時間做一次」，也就是「有時」的意思。另外還有 once in a lifetime（一生一次）、once in a blue moon（千載難逢）等說法。

---

copier = 影印機／get jammed = 〔影印紙等〕卡住／every time ~ = 每次～時／scrap paper = 用過回收的單面紙張；廢紙

「卡紙」說成 paper jam，e.g. It took me 30 minutes to print 20 pages because of paper jams.（由於卡紙，我花了 30 分鐘才印出 20 頁）

Looks like ~ =似乎～／maintenance = 維修〔部門〕

something is wrong with ~ 就是「～出了某些問題」的意思。而「〔機器〕壞了」可用 out of order，e.g. You can't use the fax machine because it's out of order.（你不能用那台傳真機，因為它壞了）

---

transmission error = 傳輸錯誤（也可用 delivery error）

「接收傳真」說成 receive a fax message。而「將～傳真出去」說成 fax ~，「傳真給～」說成 send ~ a fax。此外「撕下〔從傳真機吐出來的〕傳真紙」說成 pull the piece of paper off the fax。

---

have trouble ~ing = 做～有困難／small print = 小字

「老花眼的；遠視的」是 far-sighted， e.g. I think I'm becoming far-sighted because of my age.（由於年齡的關係，我覺得我變老花眼了）

13 我剩沒幾張印花稅票了，所以要去郵局買一些回來。

I only have a few revenue stamps in stock, so I'll go get some at the post office.

14 幫我用掛號寄送這份文件，可以嗎？

Have this document sent by registered mail, will you?

15 你一定要好好保管這份文件，因為其中包含機密（個人）資料。

Make sure you look after this document because it contains <u>classified</u> (<u>personal</u>) information.

16 最近的新進員工連電話應對都講不好。

Recruits these days can't even have a proper telephone conversation.

17 新進員工被教導，要在鈴聲響第一次時就接起電話。

New recruits are taught to pick up the phone on the first ring.

18 由於最近我們一直收到許多顧客投訴，所以光拿起電話就讓我緊張得不得了。

Since we've been having a lot of customer complaints recently, just picking up the phone gives me butterflies in my stomach.

in stock = 有存貨╱post office = 郵局

stock 是指「存貨」，故「缺貨；沒有存貨」就說成 out of stock，e.g. Staples are out of stock, so we should call the supplier.（釘書針已經沒存貨了，我們該打個電話給供應商才行）

---

have ~ sent = 寄送～╱registered mail =〔報值〕掛號信

「指定時間郵遞」說成 mail ~ at a specified time，「用快捷╱〔一般〕掛號郵件來寄～」說成 send ~ by express (certified) mail，e.g. I'd like to send this by express mail.（我想用快捷郵件來寄這個）

---

make sure S+V = 務必確認 S+V╱look after ~ = 看管～；照顧～╱classified = 機密的

「小心處理～」也可說成 handle ~ with care，e.g. Confidential data should be handled with care.（機密資料應該小心處理）

---

recruit = 新進員工╱these days = 最近╱have a telephone conversation = 用電話交談

這裡的 proper conversation 是指 business-conversation 與 private chat（私下閒聊）的要求自然不同。

---

pick up the phone = 拿起電話╱on the first ring =〔電話鈴聲〕響第一次時

on the first ring 就是「電話鈴聲響第一次時」的意思。cf. Hang up your cellphone after one ring so I can get your phone number.（手機鈴聲響一次之後就掛斷，這樣我就能取得你的電話號碼）

---

customer complaint = 顧客投訴╱give ~ butterflies in one's stomach = 令～忐忑不安

butterflies in one's stomach 直譯是「胃裡有蝴蝶飛舞的感覺」，一般用來指「心裡七上八下、忐忑不安」，e.g. I've got butterflies in my stomach.（我很緊張）

19 那通外國人突然打來的電話，真是把我嚇壞了。
That sudden phone call from a non-Chinese surprised the hell out of me.

20 要詢問我們的產品？把電話轉給業務部，讓他們去處理吧。
An inquiry about our product? Transfer the call to the sales department and let them deal with it.

21 不知道那個課的分機是幾號？
I wonder what the extension number of that section is?

22 無論我什麼時候打電話到那家公司，永遠都打不通。
No matter when I call, I can never get through to that company.

23 我今天工作很順利，感覺真好。
My job is going without a hitch today. I feel so good.

24 每個月底都有好幾個截止期限同時到。
A number of deadlines overlap at the end of every month.

non-Chinese = 非華人；外國人（此說法比 foreigner 有禮貌）／surprise the hell out of ~ = 嚇了~一大跳

hell 的原意為「地獄」，the hell [out of] 是一種強調說法，由於是較口語的用法，故最好只用在較親近的同事之間，e.g. What the hell are you talking about?（你到底在說些什麼？）

inquiry = 詢問；洽詢／transfer ~ to ... = 把~轉給…／sales department = 業務部／deal with ~ = 處理~；應付~

inquire about ~ 就是「詢問關於~」之意，e.g. I'm calling to inquire about your Internet services.（我打電話來是要詢問有關貴公司的網路服務）

I wonder ~ = 不知~／extension number = 分機號碼／section =〔較小的部門〕處；科；股；課

「〔不必花電話費的〕內線電話」說成 house phone，e.g. Please use the house phone in the meeting room to call me.（請用會議室裡的內線電話打給我）

No matter when ~ = 無論什麼時候~都／get through to ~ = 接通~；打進~

put ~ through to ... 就是「將~的電話轉到…」的意思。當你撥打公司代表號後，想拜託總機「請幫我轉到會計部」時，便可說成 Will you put me through to the accounting department?。

without a hitch = 很順利；毫無障礙

go＋副詞可表達「以~的狀態進行著」之意，e.g. Everything is going well.（一切順利）。without a hitch 是副詞片語，表示「〔工作等〕順利」，注意，hitch 指「障礙」。

a number of ~ = 一些~；多個~／deadline = 截止期限／overlap = 重疊

meet (miss) the deadline 就是「趕上（錯過）截止期限」。此外，要表達「到……截止」也可用形容詞 due（到期的）這個字來表達，例如 This report is due on Friday.（這份報告週五要交）。

25 今天瑣事不斷，真讓我喘不過氣來。
I can't catch a break with the endless parade of chores today.

26 我最好趕快把這事做完，以進行下一個任務。
I better get it over with now, and go on to the next task.

27 她的工作量已超過負荷。
She's got more work than she can manage.

28 未經我老闆同意，我是不能進行下一步的。
I can't move on to the next step without my boss's permission.

29 「在今天之內完成」他說得倒很容易，但是……
It's easy for him to say "Get this done by the end of the day," but...

30 我旁邊這傢伙自言自語得好大聲，讓我無法專心工作。
The guy next to me is talking to himself so loudly I can't concentrate on my work.

can't catch a break = 連喘氣的時間都沒有／endless parade of ~ = 一連串無止盡的～／chores = 雜務；瑣事

catch one's breath 指「屏息；喘氣」。另外，get one's second wind（獲得喘息而恢復元氣）這個說法也很常用，e.g. I got my second wind after taking a coffee break.（喝杯咖啡休息一下後，我又恢復元氣了）

I better ~ = 我最好～

get it over with 比 finish（完成）更能強烈表達「〔快快〕解決；搞定」討厭的事或麻煩的事之意。

---

manage = 勉強應付

此例句直譯成中文就是「她的工作量超過了她所能應付的程度」，而「應付」也可用 handle 這個字來表達，e.g. Let me handle this one.（這一個讓我來處理）。

---

move on to ~ = 繼續進行～／permission = 允許；同意

「請求（取得）某人的同意」說成 ask for (get) someone's approval，e.g. You have to get your boss's approval to take a vacation.（你必須取得你老闆的同意才能休假）

---

it's easy for him to ~ = 他做～是很容易的／get ~ done = 完成～／by the end of the day = 在今天結束前

「任意支使；隨心所欲地使喚～」說成 have ~ at one's beck [and call]，e.g. The boss always has his staff at his beck.（這位老闆總是任意使喚員工）。

---

talk to oneself = 自言自語／loudly = 大聲地／concentrate on ~ = 專注於～

「使煩躁」為 irritate，e.g. I was really irritated because he kept tapping his foot.（由於他一直在用腳打拍子，真的讓我很煩躁）

31 主任真的很會逃避責任。
The chief sneaks out of his duties really well.

32 只要有變動，就請通知我們。
Please inform us every time there's a change.

33 農曆年假期間，我們將照常營業。
During the Chinese new year holidays, we'll do business as usual.

34 我打算不加班完成工作。
I'm going to finish off my work without doing overtime.

35 你不能用那種收據來報帳。
You can't claim expenses with that kind of receipt.

36 把發票傳給我為何需要花這麼久時間？
Why are they taking so long to pass their invoices on to me?

sneak out of ～ = 從～偷偷逃出來；偷懶

「偷懶；摸魚」常用 goof off 這個片語來表達，e.g. I happened to catch the manager goofing off in the cafeteria.（我碰巧逮到經理在員工餐廳裡摸魚）

---

inform = 通知／every time = 每次

「一直讓～知道最新狀況；隨時向～報告情況」就説成 keep ~ informed/posted，e.g. Please keep me posted on the progress.（請隨時向我報告進度）

---

during ～ = ～期間／do business = 營業／as usual = 照常

「日曆年度（1 月 1 日～12 月 31 日）」説成 calendar year，「會計年度」則叫 fiscal year。

---

finish off ～ = 完成～／overtime = 加班時間

do/work overtime 就是「加班；超時工作」的意思。「準時下班」是 leave the office on time。另外「朝九晚五的工作」可説成 9-to-5 job。

---

claim = 要求／expenses = 費用／receipt = 收據

claim expenses 指「報帳」。「謊報費用」可説成 cheat on expenses，e.g. They say Mr. Gread often cheats on his travel expenses.（聽説葛利德先生經常謊報出差費用）

---

why = 為何／take long to ～ = 花很長時間做～／pass ~ on to ... = 把～傳給…／invoice = 發票；發貨單

「把該做的事往後延」説成 procrastinate，e.g. You shouldn't procrastinate about organizing your desk.（你不該一直拖著不整理辦公桌），而拖拖拉拉的人便説成 procrastinator。

37 發票內容有誤。我得修正它才行。

There's an error on the invoice. I should have it corrected.

38 處理錢的時候你必須更加小心才行！

You've got to be more careful when dealing with money.

39 我們現在剛好處在會計期中間，忙得我幾乎無法睡覺。

We're right in the middle of an accounting period, and it's been so hectic that I can barely sleep.

40 如果你不具備良好的電腦技能，基本上你就會被視為毫無用處。

You're basically considered useless if you don't have good computer skills.

41 有人擅長函數嗎？我正在製作 Excel 的試算表。

Is anyone good at functions? I'm working on an Excel spreadsheet now.

42 輸入電腦資料若只是偶一為之，其實也是很不錯的變化。

Inputting data on a computer is good for a change, if it's only once in a while.

have ~ corrected = 使~被修正好

「請把修正後的發票寄過來」，可寫成 Please send us the corrected invoice.，而「附件為修正後的發票」則寫成 Enclosed is a corrected invoice.。

've got to ~ (= have to) = 必須~／deal with ~ = 處理~／when dealing ~ = when you are dealing ~

「金錢往來」可説成 giving and taking money，e.g. You cannot be too careful when giving and taking money.（處理金錢往來的事情時，再小心也不為過）

---

accounting period = 會計期間／so ~ that... = 如此~以至於…／hectic = 忙亂的／can barely ~ = 幾乎無法~

「會計期間」也可説成 fiscal term。「〔忙得〕我每天都必須加班」則説成 [so hectic] that I have to work overtime every day。

---

basically = 基本上／be considered ~ = 被視為~

「在工作上有即戰力的」則用 work-ready，e.g. Generally, companies are seeking work-ready graduates.（通常企業都想找具備即戰力的畢業生）

---

function = 函數／work on ~ = 努力處理~／spreadsheet = 試算表

「擅長~」一般用 be good at ~ 來表達。「熟練的技術人員」説成 skilled technicians。

---

input = 輸入／change = 變化

for a change 可指「轉換心情」，e.g. Why don't we take a short walk around the building for a change?（我們何不繞著大樓散步，以轉換心情？）

43 我建立新系統時相當辛苦。
I had a hard time establishing the new system.

44 在辦公室內不准寄私人電子郵件。
No private e-mails in the office.

45 碰到不懂的，我就上網用 Google 搜尋！
I just google what I don't know.

46 我的電腦又不動了！我根本沒時間應付這種事！
My computer froze again! I don't have time for this!

47 不會吧！難不成我的電腦中毒了？
This can't be happening! I've got a computer virus?

48 我的電腦當機，資料都不見了。我真該把資料備份起來的。
My computer crashed and the data's gone. I should've backed it up.

have a hard time ~ing = 做～時很辛苦／establish = 建立

「做～時遇上困難」可用 have <u>difficulty/trouble</u> with ~，e.g. We had trouble with rearranging all the files.（我們重新整理所有檔案時遇上了困難）

---

private = 私人的

No ~ 就是「禁止～」之意。公告上經常出現 No ~ allowed（禁止～）這種句型，e.g. No food or drink allowed here.（此處禁止飲食）、No recording allowed.（禁止錄音）、No pets allowed.（禁止寵物）

---

google = 使用 Google 搜尋

google 這個單字是將搜尋引擎品牌 Google 轉化成動詞而成。「我輸入我想搜尋的字」說成 I type in the word I want to search for.。

---

freeze =〔電腦〕停住不動（froze 是 freeze 的過去式）

「在開機時停住不動」說成 freeze during startup；「莫名其妙就強制關機了」說成 shut down for no reason；而「伺服器掛掉了」則說成 The server has crashed.。

---

can't be ~ = 不可能～

電腦「中毒了」說成 get infected by a computer virus，而「清除電腦病毒」則說成 get rid of a computer virus。

---

should've ~ (= should have) = 應該先做好～／back ~ up = 把～備份起來

「資料無法恢復」說成 The data is irretrievable.，而「我定期備份資料」則說成 I back up the data periodically.。

49 當電子郵件伺服器掛掉時，我真不知道會發生什麼事。
When the mail server was down, I had no idea what would happen.

50 你看她指甲這麼長，打字竟然還能打得那麼快！
Look how fast she can type with such long nails!

51 不停地敲鍵盤令我肩頸僵硬。
Hammering at the keys is giving me stiff shoulders.

52 你也太落伍了吧？
How out of touch are you?

53 請不要每次電腦出問題都找我幫忙。我可不是你的電腦服務台。
Please don't ask me for help every time something's wrong with your computer. I'm not your helpdesk.

have no idea = 不知道

欲表達「（不知該怎麼辦）茫然」之意時，可用 find oneself in a stew（感覺像身處燉菜中）這種講法，e.g. He found himself in a stew because no one showed up at his presentation.（由於沒人來參加他的簡報，使得他一陣茫然）

how fast = 多麼地快速／long nails = 長指甲

「打字打得很好」説成 type well，而「用 10 隻手指打字」説成 type with all one's fingers，至於「不看鍵盤打字」則説成 type without looking at the keyboard。

hammer at ～ = 敲打～／stiff shoulders = 肩頸僵硬

「慢性的肩頸僵硬」叫 chronic stiff shoulders。

out of touch = 落伍的；脱離現實的

out of touch 原意是「沒有接觸」，在此指「不諳時事、脱離現實」，可用在包括電腦資訊等各種話題上，e.g. I'm out of touch with the latest information.（我對最新資訊一無所悉。）

ask ～ for help = 請求～幫忙／helpdesk = 提供電腦協助的服務台

I call the helpdesk to fix my computer. 就是「我打電話給電腦服務台，請人來修我的電腦」。另外「做雜事的人」可用 handyman 來表達，e.g. I don't want to be called a handyman.（我可不想被稱為是打雜的）

Skit  內勤篇

當科技宅男幫忙做一般事務時……

Woman: **This can't be happening! I've got a computer virus.**

Man: **Don't panic❶. I'll take a look at❷ it.**

W: **Oh, I've got more work than I can manage already. I still have to answer the phone and send a fax.**

M: **Can I help with❸ something?**

W: **Will you make 10 copies of the financial statements for the first quarter?**

M: **You're kidding! The copier gets jammed every time I use scrap paper.**

W: **Then don't use scrap paper.**

M: **Ha, ha, ha. Very funny.**

W: **Just clip the documents together for the meeting at 4 o'clock.**

M: **I don't know where the paper clips are.**

W: **How out of touch are you?**

M: **Hey, I'm good at❹ computers. I can reboot your computer, set up the printer and set your password, but I don't know much about general office work❺.**

W: **All right. You deal with❻ the computer. I'll make the copies.**

女子：不會吧！我的電腦中毒了。

男子：別慌張。讓我看看。

女：噢，我的工作量已超過負荷。我還得接電話並送一份傳真。

男：有什麼我能幫忙的嗎？

女：可不可以麻煩你影印 10 份第一季的財務報表。

男：妳在說笑吧！每次我用回收廢紙影印，影印機就會卡紙。

女：那就別用回收廢紙嘛。

男：哈哈哈，妳真幽默。

女：請把 4 點會議要用的文件用迴紋針夾起來就好。

男：我不知道迴紋針在哪裡耶。

女：你也太狀況外了吧？

男：嘿，我電腦很強喔。我可以幫你把電腦重開機、設定印表機，還會設定妳的密碼，但是我對一般事務工作不太了解。

女：好。那你處理電腦，我來影印。

【單字片語】

❶ panic：慌張；陷入恐慌

❷ take a look at ~：查看~；看看~

❸ help with ~：幫忙做~

❹ be good at ~：擅長~

❺ general office work：一般的辦公室工作

❻ deal with ~：處理~

Quick Check

讓我們一起來複習本章所介紹過的句型！請依據以下中文句子的意思，完成對應的英文句子。（答案就在本頁最下方）

❶ 我將來電按保留要對方等候。 →P016

I (   ) the call (   ) (   ).

❷ 我確認工作流程。 →P016

I (   ) (   ) of the (   ).

❸ 我檢討工作流程以排除不必要的工作。 →P017

I (   ) the (   ) to (   ) (   ) jobs.

❹ 我請我的主管簽核文件。 →P017

I (   ) my boss (   ) the documents.

❺ 我記錄零用金的流向。 →P018

I (   ) (   ) (   ) the (   ) cash.

❻ 我成功了！及時趕上上班時間！ →P022

I (   ) (   )! (   ) (   ) (   ) for work!

❼ 我的抽屜塞滿了舊資料。我想該整理一下了。 →P022

My drawers are (   ) (   ) (   ) (   ) old papers.
Guess (   ) (   ) (   ) (   ) them.

❽ 由於文件堆積如山，所以我今天一整天必須傾全力處理辦公室的工作。 →P022

(   ) all the documents that have (   ) (   ), I have to
(   ) (   ) (   ) office work all day today.

❾ 由於最近我們一直收到許多顧客投訴，所以光拿起電話就讓我緊張得不得了。 →P026

Since we've been having a lot of customer (   ) recently, just
(   ) (   ) the phone (   ) me (   ) in (   )
(   ).

❿ 不停地敲鍵盤令我肩頸僵硬。 →P038

(   ) (   ) the (   ) is (   ) me (   ) (   ).

---

❶put/on/hold ❷make/sure/workflow ❸ time/to/organize ❽With/piled/up/buckle/
review/workflow/eliminate/unnecessary ❹ down/to ❾complaints/picking/up/gives/
have/sign ❺keep/track/of/petty ❻made/ butterflies/my/stomach ❿Hammering/at/
it/Just/in/time ❼filled/to/capacity/with/it's/ keys/giving/stiff/shoulders

chapter 2

人際關係
Human Relationships

上司、前輩、同事、晚輩…
在辦公室生活中，
總是避不開人際關係。
在指導與被指導、
照顧與被照顧的過程中，
自言自語的機會也不少呢。

Words 單字篇

❸主管；上司（老闆）
❹副總經理
❺〔總〕經理
❻主任

❼管理階級
❽中階主管

❾同事
❿同輩；同儕

⓫辦公室戀情

❶新進員工；新
聘人員；菜鳥
❷助理

⓬同事聯姻

❶new employee/[new] recruit/rookie ❷assistant ❸chief/boss
❹deputy general manager ❺[general] manager ❻director
❼management ❽middle management ❾colleague/co-worker
❿peer ⓫office romance ⓬marriage between co-workers

首先，讓我們透過各種事、物的名稱，來掌握「人際關係」給人的整體印象。

⑬組織
⑭地位
⑮頭銜
⑯責任
⑰功勞
⑱派系
⑲派系鬥爭
⑳上司；上級
㉑下屬
㉒全體職員；員工
㉓婚外情

⑬organization ⑭position ⑮title ⑯responsibility ⑰credit
⑱faction ⑲factional fighting ⑳superior ㉑subordinate
㉒staff/staff member ㉓extramarital affair

1 我請上司指示。
I ask my boss for instructions.

2 我請上司針對我的私事提供意見。
I ask my boss for advice on personal matters.

3 我向上司抱怨工作。
I complain to my boss about my job.

4 我頂撞上司。
I talk back to my boss.

5 我討好上司。
I butter up my boss.

❶ ask ~ for ... 就是「向～請求…」之意。
❷ personal matters（私事）也可用 personal stuff 表達。
❸ complain 是「抱怨；發牢騷」之意。
❺ butter up 就是「討好」之意，而「我努力取悅上司」也可說成 I try hard to please my boss.。

tips

46 身 體 動 作 篇

6 我忍受上司發牢騷。
I endure listening to my boss's complaints.

7 我和同事處得很好。
I get along well with my <u>colleagues</u>/<u>co-workers</u>.

8 有一個同事開始讓我感到不自在。
I begin to feel uneasy with one of my <u>colleagues</u>/<u>co-workers</u>.

9 我的工作表現比同事們差。
I was left behind by my <u>co-workers</u>/ <u>colleagues</u> in performance.

10 我替我的同事收爛攤子。
I clear up my co-worker's mess.

❻ 此例句也可說成 I have to listen to my boss <u>complain</u>/<u>grumble</u>.。
❽ feel uneasy 是「感覺不自在」之意。「我發現有一個同事很難相處」說成 I find it difficult to get along with one of my <u>colleagues</u>/<u>co-workers</u>.。
❿ 此例句即 I have to cover my co-worker's mistakes.（我不得不幫忙掩蓋我同事所犯的錯）之意。

11 我為該新進員工說明工作。
I explain the job to the new employee.

12 我一對一地指導員工。
I instruct my staff members one on one.

13 我給我的員工指示。
I give instructions to my staff members.

14 我讓年輕的同事接手我的工作。
I have my younger colleague take over my job.

15 我把這工作交給我的助理。
I leave the job to my assitant.

tips

⓫ 此例句也可說成 I instruct the [new] recruit about the job procedures.。
⓬ 「一對一」一般就用 one on one 來表達。
⓭ 此例句也可說成 I tell my staff members what to do.（我告訴我的員工們該做什麼）。

16 我試著激勵我的員工。
I try to motivate my staff members.

17 我讚美（斥責）我的員工。
I praise (reprimand) my staff members.

18 我與員工們同一陣線（支持我的員工）。
I take my staff's side (stick up for my staff).

19 我偏愛某個員工。
I favor one of my staff over everyone else.

20 我把功勞讓給屬下。
I let my subordinates take the credit.

⑯ motivate 就是「激勵；給予動機」之意。

⑰ 「嚴厲地責罵」，可用 rebuke（訓斥），而若用 scold「責罵」這個字，會讓人感覺被罵的對象是小孩子。

⑲ 「我給某位員工特別待遇」就說成 I give one staff member special treatment.。

21 我傾聽員工的問題／煩惱。
I listen to my employees talk about their problems/worries.

22 我積極地去結識公司裡的人。
I actively try to get to know the people in the company.

23 我和興趣相同的同事們組成一個聯絡網。
I build a network of co-workers who have the same interests.

24 我和一位同事談戀愛（結婚）。
I get involved with (married) a colleague.

25 我跟我的上司外遇。
I have an affair with my boss.

tips

㉑ problem 指「問題」，而 worry 指「煩惱」。
㉒ get to know 是「結識」的意思。注意，此處不可只使用單字 know。
㉓ 「興趣相同的同事們」也可說成 co-workers with the same interests。
㉔ 「我愛上了我的同事」說成 I have fallen in love with my colleague.。

公司組織相關用語

股東 stockholder　　股東大會 stockholders' meeting

主管、負責人

執行長 CEO (Chief Executive Officer)
財務長 CFO (Chief Financial Officer)
營運長 COO (Chief Operating Officer)
董事長 representative director
主席 chairperson
總裁 president
副總裁 vice president
資深常務董事 senior managing director
執行董事 executive managing director
主管、幹部 executive (exec)
董事會 Board of Directors
營運總部 Operational Headquarters (OHQ)
[總]經理 [general] manager
主任 director

審計部 audit department
審計人員 auditor
主計人員 controller

秘書室 Office of Secretariat
秘書 secretary

部 Department（Dept.）／處 Division

總務部 general affairs ~
會計部 accounting ~
財務部 finance ~
法務部 legal ~
人事部 personnel/human resources ~
企劃部 planning ~
研究開發部
research & development ~
業務部 sales ~
系統部 system ~
公關部 public relations ~
製造部 manufacturing ~
物流部 logistics ~

課 Section

銷售推廣課 sales promotion ~
商品開發課 product planning ~
生產管理課 product control ~
品質管理課 quality control ~

1 我真的很幸運能在工作上擁有良好的人際關係（一位好上司）。
I'm really lucky to have <u>good personal relationships</u> (<u>a good boss</u>) at work.

2 我欠他一個人情（很多），所以沒辦法拒絕他。
I owe him <u>a favor</u> (<u>a lot</u>), so I can't say no to him.

3 我發現我很難跟那個人相處。
I find it hard to get along with that person.

4 我認為什麼事都用電子郵件聯絡是很不友善的，尤其是當對方就坐在你旁邊時。
I think it's very unfriendly to use e-mail for everything, especially when the person is sitting right next to you.

5 我試著不和同事太過親近。
I try not to get too personal with my co-workers.

6 我不想被捲入派系鬥爭。
I don't want to get <u>involved</u>/<u>caught up</u> in the factional fighting.

lucky = 幸運的／personal relationships = 人際關係／at work = 在工作上
若欲表達「我在公司的人際關係不太好」，則可説成 I don't have good personal relationships in the office.。

---

owe = 欠，e.g. I owe a lot to you. = 我欠你很多。／favor = 恩惠／say no = 說不
「拒絕」也可用 turn down（拒絕；駁回）這個片語，例如 I can't turn him down.。

---

find it hard to ~ = 發現~是很困難的（此處的 it 指其後的 to...）／get along with ~ = 與~〔和睦〕相處
欲表達對方是很難相處（難搞）的人時，可説成 That person is difficult to deal with.。

---

unfriendly = 不友善的／for everything = 對所有事務／sit right next to ~ = 就坐在~隔壁
此例句也可改成 Don't you think it's very unfriendly to use e-mail for everything...? 這種疑問句形式。

---

too~ = 太過~的／personal = 個人的；私人的／co-worker = 同事
你也可直接表達「想保持距離（keep one's distance）」之意，説成 I like to keep my distance with co-workers.。

---

get involved in ~ = 被捲入~；和~扯上關係／get caught up in ~ = 被捲入~（caught 為 catch 的過去式，也是過去分詞）／factional fighting = 派系鬥爭（faction = 派系；黨派）
「我被迫捲入派系鬥爭」就説成 I was forced to be involved in the factional fighting.。

7 來吧！你做得到的！
Come on! You can do it!

8 我真希望能在這麼能幹的上司手下做事。
I wish I could work for such a competent boss.

9 我願意在我整個職涯中都與我們的陳經理共事！
I'd like to work with our manager, Ms. Chen, throughout my career!

10 我的上司很照顧大家，所以備受尊敬。
My boss takes good care of people and so she is well respected.

11 他很懂得如何激勵他的員工。
He really knows how to motivate his staff.

12 經理看似什麼都沒有注意到，但是其實他都有在檢查細節。
The manager never seems to notice anything, but actually he is checking the details.

You can do it = 你能做到

表激勵之意除了用 Come on! 之外，還有 Don't give up!（別放棄！）、Go for it!（放手一搏！）、Keep it up!（繼續努力！）等等說法。

I wish I could ~ = 真希望我能～／work for ~ = 替～工作／such a ~ = 如此～的／competent = 能幹的；稱職的

「他工作能力很差」可說成 He is rather incompetent at work.。

I'd like to ~ = 我願意～／work with ~ = 和～共事／throughout ~ = 在整個～期間／career [kə`rɪr] =〔終生的〕事業；職涯

此例句中的 throughout my career 也可改為 all through my career。

take care of ~ = 照顧～／be well respected ~ = 備受尊敬

本例句也可說成 We respect our boss a lot because she takes good care of people.（我們很尊敬我們的主管，因為她很照顧大家）。

how to ~ = 如何～／motivate = 激勵 （motivation = 動機；動力）

「我失去了動力」可說成 I've lost my motivation.。

notice = 注意／actually = 其實；實際上／detail = 細節 e.g. in detail = 詳細地；仔細地

「你可以把詳情告訴我嗎？」說成 Could you tell me about it in detail?。

13 除了愛講冷笑話之外，他算是個好主管。
He is a good boss except for his lame jokes.

14 我從沒替如此強逼我們的主管工作過。她該多替員工著想才對。
I've never worked for a boss who pushed us so hard. She should be more considerate of the staff.

15 我認為沒有充分理由就對下屬吼叫是「職權騷擾」。
I think it's "power harassment" to yell at your subordinates without any good reason.

16 他不該在大家面前那樣說話！
He shouldn't have spoken in that way in front of everyone!

17 經理今早似乎心情不好。
The manager seems to be in a bad mood this morning.

18 我不想有個情緒化的上司。饒了我吧！
I don't want to have a boss who is moody. Give me a break!

except for ～ = 除了～之外／lame joke = 冷笑話（lame = 拙劣的；差勁的）
注意，「冷笑話」不能直譯為 cold joke。另，「雙關語」叫 pun。

I've never ～ = 我從不曾～／push ～ hard = 強逼～／be considerate of ～ = 體貼～；替～著想
此例的第二句也可說成 She should treat us more kindly.（她應該要對我們更仁慈一點）。

---

power harassment = 職權騷擾／yell = 吼叫／without any good reason = 無充分理由
power harassment 原為日式英語，但現在也和 karoshi（過勞死）一樣成為國際通用的職場用語。而「性騷擾」叫 sexual harassment。

---

shouldn't have ～ = 不該做～（針對過去已做的事）／in that way = 以那種方式／in front of ～ = 在～之前
「你早該告訴我」說成 You should have told me earlier.。

---

seem to be ～ = 似乎～／in a bad mood = 心情不好
「心情好」當然就是 in a good mood。

---

moody = 情緒化的；喜怒無常的／Give me a break! = 饒了我吧！（break = 中斷；暫停；休息）
「饒了我吧！」之意也可用 Come on!（拜託）、Not again!（別又來了）等說法來表達。

19 我老闆把我搞得心煩意亂的！
My boss gets on my nerves!

20 去它的主管！
To hell with the chief!

21 我受夠了無法下決定又總是逃避責任的上司。
I'm <u>tired</u>/<u>sick</u> of having a boss who can't make a decision and always avoids responsibility.

22 當老闆把所有決策權都交給我時，我不知所措。
I'm at a loss when the boss leaves all the decision-making to me.

23 真令人不敢相信！他把一切都交給我，卻又在最後一刻否決我？！
It's unbelievable! He left everything to me and then disapproved at the last minute!

24 我上司搶了我所有的功勞。
My boss took all the credit for my work.

get on one's nerves = 使人心煩意亂；使人神經緊張（nerves = 神經過敏；焦躁 cf. nerve = 神經；膽量 e.g. He's got a real nerve! = 他真的很有膽量！）
「我火大了」説成 I got pissed off!，而較有禮貌的説法則是 I'm upset.（我很不高興）。

To hell with ~ = 去～的；（hell = 地獄 cf. like hell = 拼命地；不顧死活地）
本例句也可説成 The hell with the chief! 但在使用這類罵人的話時，請務必注意對象和情況。另， Go to hell!（去死吧！）算是相當粗魯的罵人方式。

be tired of ~ = sick of ~ = 對～覺得受夠了／make a decision = 做出決定／avoid = 逃避／responsibility = 責任 e.g. take responsibility = 負責；承擔責任
「拿不定主意的上司」可説成 boss who can't make up his mind。

at a loss = 不知所措／leave ~ to ... = 將～交給…／decision-making = 做決策
此例中的 I'm at a loss 即 I don't know what to do（我無所適從）之意。

unbelievable = 令人難以置信的／disapprove = 不贊成；反對 cf. approve = 認可；同意／at the last minute = 在最後一刻
「我把它交給你了」説成 I'll leave it to you.，而「一切包在我身上！」則説成 Just leave it to me!。

take credit for ~ = 將～當成自己的功勞；（credit = 功績；功勞）
「我可不是為了被人稱讚才工作的」可説成 I'm not doing my job to get credit.。

25 他總是和王經理爭論。
He's always arguing with the manager, Mr. Wang.

26 身為中階主管真的很辛苦，因為你老是被夾在中間。
It's very hard to be in middle management because you're always stuck in the middle.

27 當有人在我手下做事時，我才第一次了解到身為主管的難處。
I understood the difficulty of being in charge for the first time when I had someone working under me.

28 趁老闆不在，我們來點樂子吧！
Let's have fun while the boss is away!

29 終於有比我年輕的同事了！我再也不是這裡最幼齒的了！
Finally, I have a colleague younger than me! I'm no longer the youngest worker here.

30 這些新進員工看起來真是年輕又清新。
The new <u>employees</u>/<u>recruits</u> seem so young and fresh.

argue with ~ = 和~爭論;和~爭吵;和~爭辯

「我跟經理吵了一架」說成 I had a fight with the manager.。

---

middle management = 中階主管（management = 管理階級）／stuck = 動彈不得的;被夾住的（stuck 是 stick 的過去式和過去分詞）／in the middle = 在中間

「中階主管被夾在上司與屬下之間」就說成 The middle manager is caught between superiors and subordinates.。

---

difficulty of ~ = ~的難處;~的困難／be in charge = 做負責人;做主管／for the first time = 第一次／work under ~ = 在~手下工作

「我從沒想過我上司所經歷的痛苦」可說成 I never thought about what my boss went through.。

---

have fun = 找樂子／while ~ = 趁~的時候／away = 不在;外出

俗語中的「山中無老虎，猴子稱大王」在英語裡說成 When the cat's away, the mice will play.（注意，本句中的 mice 為 mouse（老鼠）的複數。）

---

finally = 終於;總算／no longer ~ = 不再 ~

「我的位階最低」可說成 I'm at the bottom of the hierarchy/ladder.。「一般職員」則說成 a rank-and-file employee。

---

fresh = 新鮮的;新的;沒經驗的 e.g. a person fresh out of college = 一個大學剛畢業的新鮮人

「新進員工還乳臭未乾（經驗不足）」可說成 The new employees are still wet behind the ears.。

31 我認為她很適合訓練新進員工。
I think she is the right person to train the new employees.

32 我是那種被稱讚就會進步的人。
I'm the type of person who will get better by being praised.

33 他只聽命行事。
He does only what he is told.

34 我有幾個年輕的同事相當地目中無人。
Some of my younger colleagues are so defiant!

35 喂，菜鳥！別礙我的事！
Hey, rookie! Don't get in my way!

36 我不是在找新進員工的麻煩，我只是在指導他們。
I'm not picking on the new employees, just giving them guidance.

the right person to ~ = 適合做～的人／train = 訓練

「我不適任（做不來）」可說成 I'm not up to it.。

---

the type of person who ~ = 那種～類型的人／get better = 變好；進步／praise = 稱讚；表揚（praise 可作動詞或名詞用）

此例句也可說成 I'm the kind of person who will thrive on praise.（我是那種會因讚美而茁壯的人），而 thrive 就是「茁壯成長」之意。

---

what he is told = 他被告知的事

「他不聽任何人的命令」說成 He takes order from no one.。

---

younger colleague = 年輕同事／defiant = 違抗的 cf. cheeky（放肆的）、arrogant（傲慢的）、rude（無禮的）

「自作聰明、自以為是的人」叫 smart alec.，e.g. He is a real smart ales.（他真是個自以為是的傢伙）。

---

rookie = 菜鳥／get in one's way = 妨礙～

此例的第二句也可改成 Don't cause any trouble!（別惹麻煩！）。另，亦可用 new guy 來稱呼「新人」。

---

pick on = 找碴兒／new employee = 新進員工／guidance = 指導

此例句也可說成 I'm not being mean to the new employees, only instructing them.，而句中的 mean 是指「刻薄的；心懷惡意的」。

37 如果你以為你可以躲過一切，那就大錯特錯了。
If you think you can get away with anything, you are wrong.

38 她總是很開朗，所以你可以很容易地請她做事。
She is always cheerful so you can easily ask her to do something.

39 她為辦公室帶來活力。
She brightens up the office.

40 他能以不著痕跡的方式展現他的貼心。
He can be attentive in a very subtle way.

41 李小姐是這辦公室裡值得信賴的人。
Ms. Lee is someone we can count on in the office.

42 他於公於私都是個完美男人！
He is a perfect guy both personally and professionally!

get away with ~ = 僥倖逃過~／wrong = 錯誤的

「他什麼都沒做竟然可以矇混過關」說成 He got away with doing nothing.。

---

cheerful = 開朗的；爽朗的／easily = 輕鬆地；容易地

此例句也可說成 She is such a cheerful person that you can always ask her to do something.

---

brighten up ~ = 為~增添活力 cf. bright = 明亮的；開朗的

此例句也可說成 She makes everyone feel happy in the office. 或 She cheers up everyone in the office.（她使辦公室裡的每個人都很開心。）。

---

attentive =〔對人〕用心的；〔對人〕體貼的／in a subtle way = 以不著痕跡的方式（subtle [`sʌtl] = 微妙的；精緻的）

此例句也可說成 He is considerate/thoughtful in a very casual way.，句中 considerate 是「善解人意的」、thoughtful 是「體貼的」之意，而 casual [`kæʒʊəl] 則指「隨意的」。

---

someone we can ~ = 我們可以~的人／count on ~ = 信賴~；指望~

「我總是能信賴你」就說成 I can always count on you.。

---

perfect = 完美的／both A and B = A 和 B 兩方面都／personally = 個人地；就個人而言／professionally = 在工作上；在專業上

「公私分明」可說成 draw a line between public/professional and private/personal lives，而 draw a line between ~ and ... 指「在~和…之間畫線」。

43 他總是對上司阿諛奉承，但是對下屬卻十分冷淡。
He always kisses up to his superiors but is very cold to his subordinates.

44 他這個人共事還好，但就個人而言，我並不想和他有瓜葛。
He's OK to work with, but I don't want to deal with him personally.

45 你不覺得我們公司同事聯姻的很多嗎？
Don't you think we have a lot of marriages between co-workers at this company?

46 我是同輩中唯一還沒結婚的！
I'm the only one who is not married among my peers!

47 我一直都很希望能因結婚而離職。
I've always wanted to get married and leave the company.

48 我真不敢相信他們竟然還禁止辦公室戀情。
I can't believe they still forbid office romance.

kiss up to ~ = 對～阿諛奉承 cf. butter up to~（討好～）、suck up to（拍～馬屁）/superior = 上司/subordinate = 下屬

「諂媚、阿諛、奉承」也可用單字 flatter 來表達，e.g. Don't try to flatter me because it won't work.（別想諂媚我，因為沒有用。）

---

work with ~ = 和～一起工作/deal with ~ = 和～相處；應付～

此例後半句也可說成 I don't want to get involved with him personally.，而 get involved with ~ 就是「和～有瓜葛」之意。

Don't you think~? = 你不覺得～嗎？/marriage between ~ = ～之間的婚姻

「他跟我的一個同事結婚」說成 He is married to a college of mine.。

---

the only one = 唯一的一個/be married = 已婚的/among ~ = 在～之中/peer = 同儕；同輩 e.g. peer pressure = 同儕壓力

注意，「結婚」通常用被動形式來表達，如本句中的 be married 或下句中的 get married；若用主動式則指「娶」或「嫁」，e.g. He is going to marry the boss's daughter.（他將娶老闆的女兒為妻）。

I've always wanted to ~ = 我一直都很想～/get married = 結婚/leave the company = 離職

「他因懷孕而被迫辭職」說成 She was forced to quit her job because she was pregnant.。

I can't believe ~ = 我真不敢相信～/forbid = 禁止/office romance = 辦公室戀情

「我不想和同事談戀愛」可說成 I don't want to get involved in a relationship with a co-worker.。

商務環境中的重要禮儀及表達方式

雖說商務環境中的會話可能因國家、文化不同而有差異，不過基本上，只要採取正式的表達方式並注意禮貌，應該就錯不了。

1. 在正式場合與人初次會面

在正式場合遇到初次見面的人時，可用 (It's) nice to meet you.、I'm <u>pleased/very glad</u> to meet you.（很高興認識你）等句子來打招呼。而與對方握手時，一定要看著對方的臉（眼睛）並緊握其手。尤其在美國，男性握手時若力道太輕，便很難獲得對方的信任。另外在歐美並不很流行交換名片（exchanging business cards），像日本人那種一見面就交換名片的習慣，在歐美不見得行得通，這點請務必注意。

自我介紹時，可用 <u>I am/My name is</u> Yijun Chang.（我是張怡君）這種說法，以全名來介紹自己。至於與所屬公司相關之資訊，則可用 I work for A Company.（我在 A 公司工作）、I work in the <u>sales</u> (<u>accounting</u>) department.（我在業務（會計）部工作）等方式說明。

一般來說，稱呼對方時應用尊稱（Mr./Ms.）加姓氏（last name），例如：Mr. Chou、Ms. Chen。若是在較不正式的場合中稱呼關係較親近的人，便可用名字（first name），例如：Yijun、Alex 等。尤其在美國，大家特別愛用名字相稱，但千萬注意，不可在名字之前加上尊稱（× Mr. Alan、× Ms. Audrey）。另外，在台灣經常會用「主任」、「經理」等頭銜來稱呼上司，可是英語不用這類職務名稱來稱呼人，一般會用其姓氏加尊稱來處理，例如：Mr. Spader、Ms. Schmidt。

2. 交談時的禮儀及彬彬有禮的表達方式

接著，和對方說話時，一定要注意眼神的交流（eye contact）。在適當時機答腔也很重要，但若想表達中文「是」之意而都用「Yes」來答腔，有時會變成完全同意對方所說的內容（Yes, I totally agree.），而引起誤會。故最好使用在意義上為中性的答腔用詞，如 uh-huh、I see 等，會比較保險。

荒井貴和 Text by Kiwa Arai

　　英語裡也有能表示客氣或較有禮貌的表達方式。其中最具代表性的就是使用 would、could、may、might 等助動詞。例如想拜託對方時，若直接用命令句加 please，有時會給人高傲無禮的印象（如 Answer the phone, please!（請接電話！））。若想較有禮貌，就可以說 Could you answer the phone?（能不能麻煩您接個電話？）。

　　至於自己想做某事的時候，則可利用 I'd/ I like to ~（我想～）這種句型，例如 I'd like to propose a toast.（我想提議乾杯）。

　　另外像是 Do you mind ~?（你介意～嗎？）、I'm afraid ~（我恐怕～）、if I may（如果我可以的話）等也都是很有禮貌的表達方式，可運用於各種情境，請務必牢記並加以應用。

　　而在輕鬆的會話裡，經常出現許多省略或較口語的表達方式（如：I wanna ~、I'm gonna ~、kinda、Yeah、Thanks! 等），這些都不適用於正式場合。在正式場合中務必把話說得完整（如：I want to ~、I'm going to ~、kind of ~、Yes、Thank you.）。最後，記得在商務環境或正式場合中萬萬不可爆粗口，使用像 shit、fuck 等這類髒話。

Skit  人際關係篇

中階主管之苦水吐不完

Man: **I wish I could work for such a competent boss. You're lucky.**

Woman: **He takes good care of people, so we respect him. He's a good boss except for his lame jokes.**

M: **My boss gets on my nerves. I have to endure listening to his complaints. He can't make decisions and always avoids responsibility. But he can be attentive in a very subtle way.**

W: **Well, at least❶ you really know how to motivate your people.**

M: **I try. I praise them and stick up for them, and I let them take credit for what they do.**

W: **It's hard to be in middle management because we're always stuck in the middle.**

M: **Don't give up❷. We can do it.**

男子：我真希望能在這麼能幹的上司手下做事。妳真幸運。

女子：他很照顧大家，所以我們都很尊敬他。除了愛講冷笑話外，他算是個好老闆。

男：我老闆就讓我神經緊張。我得忍受聽他發牢騷。他常無法下決定，又總是逃避責任。不過他倒是能以不著痕跡的方式展現他的貼心。

女：嗯，至少你很懂得如何激勵下屬。

男：我盡量啦。我會讚美他們、支持他們，也將屬於他們的功勞歸於他們。

女：身為中階主管真的很辛苦，因為我們老是被夾在中間。

男：別放棄！我們做得到的！

【單字片語】

❶ at least：至少
❷ give up：放棄

Quick Check

讓我們一起來複習本章所介紹過的句型！請依據以下中文句子的意思，完成對應的英文句子。（答案就在本頁最下方）

❶ 我討好上司。 →P046

I ( ) ( ) my boss.

❷ 我的工作表現比同事們差。 →P047

I was ( ) ( ) by my colleagues in ( ) ( ).

❸ 我讓讓年輕的同事接手我的工作。 →P048

I have my younger colleague ( ) ( ) my job.

❹ 我欠他一個人情，所以沒辦法拒絕他。 →P052

I ( ) him a ( ), so I can't ( ) ( ) to him.

❺ 我發現我很難跟那個人相處。 →P052

I ( ) ( ) ( ) ( ) ( ) ( )
( ) that person.

❻ 我不想被捲入派系鬥爭。 →P052

I don't want to ( ) ( ) ( ) the ( )
( ).

❼ 我不想有個情緒化的上司。饒了我吧！ →P056

I don't want to have a boss who is ( ). ( ) ( )
( ) ( )!

❽ 當老闆把所有決策權都交給我時，我不知所措。 →P058

I'm ( ) ( ) ( ) when the boss ( ) all the
( ) to us.

❾ 喂，菜鳥！別礙我的事兒！ →P062

Hey, ( )! Don't ( ) ( ) ( ) ( )!

❿ 她為辦公室帶來活力。 →P064

She ( ) ( ) the office.

---

❶butter/up ❷left/behind/business/
performance ❸take/over ❹owe/favor/
say/no ❺find/it/hard/to/get/along/with ❻
get/involved/in/factional/fighting ❼moody/

Give/me/a/break ❽at/a/loss/
decision-making ❾rookie/get/in/my/way ❿
brightens/up

72

chapter 3

業務員
Salesperson

外出拚業績、
向客戶說明產品與服務、
還要議價協商，
業務員追求數字目標、背負利潤使命，
行動時充滿鬥志，
內心卻也偶有低語。

Words 單字篇

❶業務員

❷外出跑業務

❽第一印象
❾推銷辭令
❿閒聊

⓫職業笑容

❺顧客／
客戶
❻承辦人

❼名片

❸〔未經預約〕
直接登門推銷
❹定期推銷

❶salesperson ❷sales round ❸walk-in sales ❹regular sales
❺customer/client ❻person in charge ❼business card
❽first impression ❾sales talk ❿small talk ⓫business smile

首先，讓我們透過各種事、物的名稱，來掌握「業務員」給人的整體印象。

㉓銷售業績
⑳銷售紀錄
㉑銷售目標數字
㉒銷售配額
⑬產品
⑫上座
⑱合約
⑲交易
⑭估價
⑮價格
⑯交貨日期
⑰商業條款

⑫seat of honor ⑬product ⑭estimate ⑮price ⑯delivery date ⑰business terms ⑱contract ⑲deal ⑳sales record ㉑numerical sales target ㉒sales quota ㉓sales performance

1　我直接登門推銷。
I do walk-in sales.

2　我和某人交換名片。
I exchange business cards with someone.

3　我拜訪客戶後直接回家。
I visit a client and go home right after.

4　我陪我的員工去跑業務推銷產品。
I accompany my staff making the rounds to sell the product.

5　我隨身攜帶一些樣品。
I bring some samples with me.

tips

❶ walk-in 為名詞，代表「〔未經預約的〕不速之客」之意，e.g. No walk-ins.（謝絕未預約者）
❹「逐一拜訪客戶」就說成 make the rounds of my customers。
❺「〔促銷用的〕免費樣品」說成 giveaway 或 freebie。
❻「道歉」也可說成 make an apology。

6　我去拜訪客戶，為我的錯誤道歉。
I call on a client and apologize for my mistake.

7　我做新年拜訪。
I make New Year's calls.

8　我檢查儀容。
I check my appearance.

9　我檢查口氣是否清新。
I check my breath.

10　我臉上維持〔職業〕笑容。
I keep a [business] smile on my face.

❼ 此處 call 是指「〔簡短的〕拜訪」。
❽「整理儀容」、「打扮整齊」可說成 I spruce myself up.。
❾ 用 keep one's mouth odor-free 可表達「保持口氣清新」之意。

11 我開發新客戶。
I seek new customers.

12 我打推銷電話。
I make sales calls.

13 我做推銷宣傳。
I make a sales pitch.

14 我介紹新的服務。
I explain a new service.

15 我研究我的客戶。
I do research on my client.

tips

⓫ 此例句也可說成 I cultivate new customers。
⓬ 此處的 call 指「電話」。「冷不防的推銷電話」說成 cold call。
⓭ pitch ~ to ... 為「將～推銷給……」之意，e.g. We'll pitch the product to pregnant mothers.（我們將該產品推銷給孕婦）。
⓯ 「了解客戶需求」就說成 understand the client's needs。

16 我估價。
I make an estimate.

17 我議價。
I negotiate a price.

18 我訂定商業條款。
I set the business terms.

19 我以推銷辭令和客戶協商。
I negotiate with a client while giving a sales talk.

20 我提出備案。
I offer an alternative proposal/a backup plan.

⑯ 「估價單；報價單」是 quotation。
⑰ 「討價還價」說成 haggle over the price，e.g. I haggled over the price with the shop owner.（我和商店老闆討價還價）。
⑱ term 是「條件」之意，e.g. payment terms（付款條件）、loan terms（貸款條件）。

21 我仔細檢查交貨日期。
I double-check the delivery date.

22 我向上司確認。
I check with my boss.

23 我簽署合約。
I sign a contract.

24 我檢查銷售紀錄。
**I check the
sales record.**

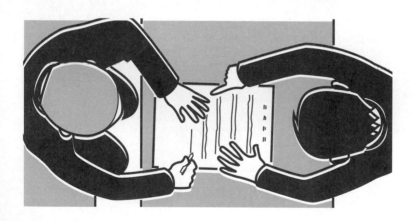

tips

㉑ double-check 是「重複檢查；仔細檢查」之意。

㉒ check with ~ 就是「詢問～以確認」。而 check~ against... 指「核
對…以確認～」e.g. I check the report against the data.（我核對
資料以確認報告無誤）

㉕「交際費」説成 entertainment expenses。

25 我款待客戶。
I entertain a client.

26 我修改銷售目標數字。
I revise the numerical sales target.

27 我做出成果。
I achieve a result.

㉖「設定目標數字」說成 set a numerical target，e.g. We set numerical targets for the reduction of office trash.（我們替辦公室垃圾減量設定了目標數字）

1 那個客戶總是態度非常謹慎，光約個時間都很難。
That client always has a guarded attitude so it's really tough just to make an appointment.

2 不知那個客戶現在是否有空。
I wonder if the client is available now.

3 怎麼會呢！最後我們竟然重複下單！
No way! We ended up double-booking!

4 我的客戶在最後一刻取消了約定。
I got canceled on by a client at the last minute.

5 我的名片快用完了。我得補足才行。
I'm running short of my business cards. I've got to top them up.

6 那位承辦人員對所有事情都一絲不苟，所以你要注意禮貌。
The person in charge there is meticulous about everything, so mind your P's and Q's.

guarded = 小心的；謹慎的／attitude = 態度／tough = 棘手的／make an appointment = 預約

take a guarded stance to ~ 就是「對～採取謹慎的立場」，e.g. I feel they always take a guarded stance to us.（我覺得他們對我們總是採取謹慎的立場）

I wonder if ~ = 不知是否～

available 就是「〔人〕有空」的意思。「〔在日期時間上〕方便」則用 convenient，e.g. Is Tuesday at 2 p.m. convenient for you?（週二下午 2 點你方便嗎？）

No way! = 怎麼可能！／end up ~ = 結果是～

要表達「怎麼可能！」可說成 This can't be happening!，e.g. All the data's gone? This can't be happening!（所有的資料都不見了？怎麼可能！）

---

get canceled on = 被取消／at the last minute = 在最後一刻

「在最後關頭退出」可說成 back out at the last minute，e.g. Mr. Doncam said he'd come to the year-end party but he backed out at the last minute.（唐肯先生說他會來參加尾牙，但是卻在最後一刻打了退堂鼓）

---

be running short of ~ = ～快要沒有了／top ~ up = 補滿～

be short of ~ 就是「～不足；缺乏～」的意思，e.g. I'm sorry. I'm short of cash.（很抱歉，我的現金不足）

---

meticulous = 一絲不苟的／mind one's P's and Q's = 注意禮貌

P's and Q's 指 "please" 和 "excuse me"（「請」和「對不起」，即「禮貌」之意）。而其他有用到英文字母的有趣說法，還包括 dot the i's and cross the t's（別忘了 i 上面的點和 t 的那一橫），亦即「請小心注意」之意。

7　夏天跑業務令我汗流浹背。
Making sales rounds in the summer makes me sweat.

8　我要給我的客戶強烈的第一印象。
I'm going to make a strong first impression on my client.

9　你應該知道，良好的第一印象最為重要。
You should know a good first impression is everything.

10　他現在不在？那我留個名片好了。
He's not in now? Then I'll just leave my card.

11　我想首先我自己應該要喜歡產品才行。
I guess I should love the product myself first.

12　身為業務員，你不能光講自己的事，應該要詢問客戶需求。
As a salesperson, you shouldn't talk only about yourself but ask your client what he wants.

sales round = 外出跑業務／sweat = 流汗

「內勤；辦公室工作」可用 <u>desk/office</u> work，e.g. I did nothing but desk work today.（我今天都只做辦公室內的工作）。而「今天真是個大熱天」可說成 It's sweltering hot today.。

make an impression on ~ = 讓～留下印象

「認得～的臉」說成 know ~ by sight，e.g. I know him by sight but don't remember his name.（我認得他的臉，但是不記得他的名字）

You should know~ = 你應該知道，～／be everything = 最為重要

「最要緊的是～；最重要的是～」可用 What counts most is ~ 來表達，e.g. What counts most is leading a healthy life.（最重要的是要過健康的生活）

be not in = 不在〔公司〕／leave ~ = 將～留下

要表達「承辦人員目前不在，你想留個言嗎？」之意時，可說 The person in charge is not in now. Would you like to leave a message?。

I guess ~ = 我想～／first = 首先

「喜歡上～」可用 take to ~ 來表達，e.g. She took to our products when they were introduced on TV.（當我們的產品上電視時，她就喜歡上那些產品了）

salesperson (= sales representative) = 業務員／client = 客戶

「良好的傾聽技巧」說成 good listening skills，e.g. Learning good listening skills is vital for sales representatives.（學習良好的傾聽技巧，對業務員而言極為重要）

13 由於我必須和客戶閒聊，所以我應該要能時時接受新思維。

Since I need to make small talk with clients, I should always keep myself open to new ideas.

14 只去我的老客戶那邊做定期的業務拜訪，沒什麼用處。

Just making regular sales visits to my regular clients is not rewarding.

15 我最好別忘了對新的承辦人員好好介紹一下我們的產品。

I better not forget to do a good demonstration of our products to the new person in charge.

16 那個位置是上座嗎？

Is the spot over there the seat of honor?

17 我不知道何時該開始喝人家端給我的茶。

I don't know when to start drinking the tea served to me.

18 看來他們對產品很滿意。也許我可以開始推銷了。

Looks like they like the product a lot. Maybe I can go ahead with the sale.

make small talk with ～ = 和～閒聊／keep oneself open to ～ = 對～敞開心胸；願意接受～

「具有強烈的好奇心」可說成 have a great deal of curiosity，e.g. Ms. Nozey has a great deal of curiosity about everything happening in the office.（娜茲小姐對辦公室裡發生的一切都充滿了好奇心）

regular sales visit to ～ = 去～做定期的業務拜訪／regular client = 老顧客／rewarding = 有報酬的；有益的

「定期推銷」，也可說成 routine sales visits，e.g. I'm bored with my routine sales visits.（我對我的例行性業務拜訪感到很厭倦）

better not ～ = 最好別～／do a demonstration = 做〔產品〕介紹；／person in charge = 承辦人

「招徠顧客；兜售」可用 tout 表達，e.g. You don't have to tout your product. It sells itself.（你不必兜售你的產品。這產品本身就很暢銷）

spot = 位置；地點／the seat of honor = 上座；上位

「坐上座」可說成 take the head of the table，e.g. I wonder who's going to take the head of the table tonight.（我很好奇今晚誰會坐最上座）

when to ～ = 何時該～／served to ～ = 提供給～的

serve ～ to ... 是「提供～〔食物、飲料等〕給…」的意思，e.g. I serve tea to a client.（我端茶給客戶）。

look like ～ = 看來～／go ahead with ～ = 開始進行～

「從～獲得正面回應」說成 receive a positive response from ～，e.g. Our online service has been receiving positive responses from shoppers.（我們的線上服務一直都獲得了消費者正面的回應）

19 稍後我回辦公室會好好考慮你們的出價。
I'll think over your offer in the office later.

20 那個女性承辦員如此刻薄真令我難以置信！
I couldn't believe the lady in charge was so mean!

21 海山貿易公司的史派德先生是個談判高手，所以我得全力以赴才行。
Mr. Spader from Seamount trading company is a tough negotiator, so I'm going to give it all I've got.

22 和那些老客戶談話很輕鬆，因為我很了解他們。
It's easy talking with those old clients because I know them inside out.

23 不論再怎麼熟，現在的人是不會輕易給你工作的。
People won't offer you a job that easily these days, no matter how close you are to them.

24 在我看來，每個客戶都對這商品有著濃厚的興趣。
As I see it, every client takes a strong interest in this merchandise.

think over ~ = 仔細考慮～／offer = 出價；報價

「當場決定」，說成 decide on the spot，e.g. I'm afraid we can't decide on the spot.（我們恐怕無法當場決定）

---

couldn't believe = 無法置信／mean = 刻薄的；壞心腸的

How <u>can</u>/<u>could</u> ~? 是具有「～怎麼能〔當然不可以〕」這種意涵的疑問句型，e.g. How could you say that to your colleague?（你怎麼能對你的同事說那種話？）

---

trading company = 貿易公司／tough negotiator = 談判高手

give it all one's got 就是「把所有能耐全使出來」，即「盡全力」的意思，而 give it one's all 也能表達同樣意義，e.g. Give it your all!（全力以赴！）

It's easy to V/Ving = 做～很容易／know ~ inside out = 非常了解～

Inside out 原意是「裡朝外地」，有「完全」、「徹底」之意。另，upside down 指「顛倒的」、「倒置的」。

---

offer = 提供／no matter how ~ (= however ~) = 不論怎麼～；無論有多～

「因工作而認識的人」說成 business acquaintance，e.g. In this cold world, business acquaintances won't be of much help in finding a job.（在這個冷酷的世界上，因工作而認識的人對找工作來說沒什麼幫助）

---

as I see it = 在我看來／take an interest in ~ = 對～有興趣／merchandise = 商品

「對～有興趣」亦可說成 be interested in ~，e.g. I'm not interested in this subject.（我對這個科目沒有興趣）

25 我就知道他們只讓賣得快的商品上架。
I knew they'd only allow fast-selling items on the shelf.

26 唉，真令人沮喪！競爭對手的產品顯然比我們的更搶眼。
Argh, how frustrating! Obviously, our rival's product is more eye-catching than ours.

27 我想可能是因為經濟不景氣，近來顧客把荷包掐得越來越緊了。
I think it's probably because of the economic downturn, but customers these days keep a tight hold on their purse strings.

28 強迫別人購買你的東西，只會遭到拒絕而已。
You'll only get rejected if you press someone to buy your stuff.

29 你不能只是拼命賣產品，好的後續服務也同樣重要。
You can't just sell the products; you should give the same importance to good follow-through service.

30 接手這麼大的客戶，對我來說負擔太大。
Taking over such a big client is too big a burden for me.

allow = 允許／fast-selling = 賣得快的；熱銷的／item = 商品；項目

「〔商品、庫存、來客等的〕迴轉率」可用 turnover 表達，e.g. This coffee shop has good customer turnover.（這家咖啡廳的來客迴轉率很高）

Argh = 唉！啊～／how frustrating = 多令人沮喪／obviously = 明顯地／rival's product = 競爭對手的產品／eye-catching = 搶眼的；醒目的

「引人注目的事物（商品）」可說成 eye-catcher，e.g. I believe this is going to be the eye-catcher for today's event.（我相信這將成為今天活動中最搶眼的商品）

---

economic downturn (= recession) = 經濟不景氣；經濟衰退／keep a tight hold on one's purse strings = 把荷包掐得緊緊的

相反地，「鬆開荷包」說成 loosen one's purse strings。另外，「掌控荷包；掌握經濟大權」則說成 control the purse strings，e.g. My wife controls the purse strings.（我太太掌握著經濟大權）

---

get rejected = 被拒絕；被排斥／press ~ to ... = 強迫～做…

「強迫推銷」叫做 hard sell，e.g. Giving people the hard sell is never the best tactic.（強迫推銷從來都不是最上策）

---

give importance to ~ = 重視～／follow-through service = 後續服務

「售後服務」為 after-sale service。

---

take over ~ = 接手～；接管～／too big a burden = 過重的負擔

「接任～職務」可用 take over as ~ 表達，e.g. As of April 1st, Mr. Uhlman will take over as accounting director.（自 4 月 1 日起，伍爾曼先生便將接任會計主任一職）

31 這筆生意恐怕也會被法克森公司搶走吧。
I'm afraid this deal will be carried off by Foxen Inc.

32 我若能成功搞定這案子，應該會是筆大生意。
It's going to be a really big deal if I get it all sewn up.

33 我認真完成了報價。希望一切順利。
I buckled down and finished up the estimate. I hope it's all right.

34 不計任何代價，我都必須讓他們向我下單。
Whatever it takes, I must get them to place the order with me.

35 我拿到了一筆大生意的合約，感覺真棒！
I got a big sales contract, and I'm feeling on top of the world!

36 太好了！現在我是上半年的銷售冠軍了！
Yes! Now I'm the top salesperson for the first half of the year!

carry ~ off = 劫持；獲得～

「把～突然奪走」可用 swoop away ~ 表達，e.g. The manager came in and swooped away the document from under my nose. （經理進門來，在我面前把文件突然奪走）

---

deal = 生意；交易／get ~ sewn up = 成功搞定～（sewn [son] 為 sew [so] 的過去分詞，而 sew 的過去式為 sewed [sod]）

sew 的原意為「縫製」，而 sew up ~ 指「成功搞定～」。另外，也使用 deal 這個字的 It's a deal. （一言為定；成交）這種說法相當常見。

---

buckle down = 傾全力／finish up ~ = 完成～／estimate = 報價；估價

注意，buckle up 指「繫好安全帶」。

---

whatever it takes = 不計一切代價／get ~ to ... = 讓～做…／place an order with ~ = 向～下單

「無論如何」可用 whatever happens 表達，e.g. Whatever happens, I'm going to get their agreement. （無論如何，我都要取得他們的同意）

---

contract = 合約／feel on top of the world = 感覺真棒；極度開心

可表達「非常高興、感覺真棒」的說法很多，而 be on cloud nine （彷彿置身九霄雲上）、be in seventh heaven （宛如置身七重天）這兩種都源於宗教，也都用了數字，相當有意思。

Yes! = 真棒！；太好了！／salesperson = 業務員；銷售人員／the first half of the year = 上半年

「銷售業績」可說成 sales performance，e.g. I got No. 1 in annual sales performance. （我獲得了年度銷售業績的冠軍）

37 這次我沒能談成，但是至少這次的協商給了我下一回合的線索。

I couldn't pull it off this time, but at least the negotiation gave me a clue for the next round.

38 我認為她具備了做業務的必要特質，因為她和每個人都相處融洽。

I think she's got what it takes to be a salesperson because she gets along with everybody.

39 我每週六和週日都要陪客戶打高爾夫球。我再也受不了了。

I'm taking clients golfing every Saturday and Sunday. I can't take it anymore.

40 管理階層最近刪減了經費，現在我得在預算吃緊的情況下工作。

Recently, management has cut expenses, and I have to work on a strict budget now.

41 本季的銷售配額被設定得這麼高，我不知能否達成。

The sales quota this quarter is set so high I wonder if I can meet it.

42 優秀的業務員就是能夠銷售賣得不好的商品的業務員。

A good salesperson is one who sells things that don't sell themselves.

pull ~ off = 做成~／at least = 至少／clue for ~ = ~的線索／next round =
下一回合

「談成生意」還有更正式的講法，如 clinch a deal 或 conclude a bargain，
e.g. We concluded a bargain with Ternip Inc. last week.（上週我們和塔尼普
公司談成了一筆生意）

what it takes to ~ = 做~的必要條件、特質等／get along with ~ = 和~相處
〔融洽〕

「迎合所有人的需求」可説成 be all things to all people，e.g. I can't be all
things to all people.（我無法迎合所有人的需求）

take ~ golfing = 帶~去打高爾夫球／can't take it = 無法忍受；受不了

可表達「無法忍受」、「受夠了」等之意的説法還有 I can't bear/stand it.（我
無法忍受）、I've had it.（我受夠了）、I'm at my breaking point.（我快崩潰
了）、This is the last straw.（這是最後一根稻草〔我忍無可忍了〕） 等。

management = 管理階層／cut expenses = 刪減經費／on a strict budget =
在預算吃緊的情況下

「極度縮減開支」可用 to the bone（入骨地〔極端地〕）來表達，e.g. They
are cutting expenses to the bone.（他們大砍經費）

sales quota = 銷售配額／quarter = 季／I wonder if ~ = 不知能否~／meet
~ = 達成~；符合~

quota 是「分配量；配額」之意，e.g. Though it was tough, I managed to
fulfill my quota.（雖然很辛苦，但是我還是設法達到了我的配額）

sell oneself =〔放著不管也能〕自然賣得好

「賣不掉的貨品」可説成 unsellable goods 或 unmarketable products，e.g.
They say there are several ways to turn unsellable goods into salable ones.
（聽説有幾種辦法能將賣不掉的貨品變成賣得掉的貨品）。

Skit 業務員篇

銷售冠軍大方傳授 「做業務的訣竅」

Woman: I'm new to the sales department❶. I have to meet clients and tell them about our new products, but I'm nervous❷.

Man: Well, I was the top salesperson for the first half of the year. I got a big sales contract and I'm feeling on top of the world. I think I can help you.

W: I know I should always check my appearance and my breath. What else?

M: A good first impression is everything, you know. You should try to make a strong impression on your clients. And you shouldn't talk only about yourself, but ask your clients what they want.

W: That's good advice.

M: You should know a salesperson is one who sells things that don't sell themselves. Here's❸ another trick❹ I learned. The catalog is not enough. I always bring some samples with me to give to the client❺. They like that.

W: Thank you so much! I feel much more confident❻ now.

女子：我剛到業務部。我必須去見客戶並介紹我們的新產品，但是我好緊張。

男子：嗯，我是今年上半年的銷售冠軍。我拿到一筆大生意的合約，感覺真棒！我想我應該能幫妳。

女：我知道我應該要時時檢查儀容，和口氣是否清新。除此之外還有什麼呢？

男：妳也知道，良好的第一印象是最重要的。妳應該試著給客戶強烈的第一印象。另外，妳不能光講自己的事，應該要詢問客戶需求。

女：真是很好的建議。

男：妳應該知道，優秀的業務員就是能夠銷售賣得不好的商品的業務員。我還學到了另一個訣竅。那就是光靠型錄是不夠的。我總會隨身帶一些樣品送給客戶。他們都很愛。

女：真是太謝謝你了！我現在覺得有自信多了。

【單字片語】

❶ sales department：業務部
❷ nervous：緊張的
❸ Here's ~.：（我）這兒有～。
❹ trick：訣竅；花招；手法
❺ client：顧客；客戶

❻ confident：有自信的

Quick Check

讓我們一起來複習本章所介紹過的句型！請依據以下中文句子的意思，完成對應的英文句子。（答案就在本頁最下方）

❶ 我直接登門推銷。 →P076
I do ( ) ( ).

❷ 我進行新年拜訪。 →P077
I ( ) New Year's ( ).

❸ 我做推銷宣傳。 →P078
I ( ) a sales ( ).

❹ 怎麼會呢！最後我們竟然重複下單！ →P082
( ) ( )! We ( ) ( ) double-booking!

❺ 我的名片快用完了。我得補足才行。 →P082
I'm ( ) ( ) ( ) my ( ) ( ). I've got
to ( ) them ( ).

❻ 由於我必須和客戶閒聊，所以應該要時時接收新思想才好。 →P086
Since I need to ( ) ( ) ( ) with clients, I should
always ( ) ( ) ( ) to ( ) ( ).

❼ 稍後我回辦公室會好好考慮你們出的價。 →P088
I'll ( ) ( ) this offer in the office ( ).

❽ 和那些老客戶談話很輕鬆，因為我很了解他們。 →P088
It's ( ) ( ) with those ( ) clients because I know
( ) ( ) ( ) ( ).

❾ 唉，真令人沮喪！競爭對手的產品顯然比我們的更搶眼。 →P090
Argh, how ( )! Obviously, our ( ) product is more
( ) than ours.

❿ 管理階層最近刪減了經費，現在我得在預算吃緊的情況下工作。 →P094
Recently, management has ( ) ( ), and I have to work
( ) ( ) ( ) ( ) now.

---

❶walk-in/sales ❷ make/calls ❸make/pitch
❹No/way/ended/up ❺running/short/of/
business/cards/top/up ❻make/small/talk/
keep/myself/open/new/ideas ❼think/over/

later ❽easy/talking/old/them/inside/out
❾frustrating/rival's/eye-catching ❿cut/
expenses/on/a/strict/budget

chapter 4
出差
Business Trips

上班族出差的機會不算少，
事先做好準備，再踏上未知的土地，
接著滿心期待能做出成果。
若狀況允許，也可順便觀光。
身處不同環境，
新鮮事物令人目不暇給，
而腦袋也可能會轉個不停！

Words 單字篇

❶打包行李　❷住宿　❸機票
❹航班　❺高鐵
❻對號座　❼自由座
❽時令便當

❿〔投幣〕置物櫃

❾行李

⓫商務旅館
⓬電話叫醒服務

❶packing　❷accommodation　❸air ticket　❹flight　❺high-speed
railway　❻reserved seat　❼unreserved seat　❽seasonal lunch box
❾baggage　❿[coin] locker　⓫business hotel　⓬wake-up call

首先，就讓我們透過各種事、物的名稱，來掌握「出差」給人的整體印象。

⑭參觀工廠
⑮企業宣傳小冊
⑯總公司
⑰分公司
⑱樣品
⑲人脈

⑬時程表；進度表

⑳當地美食

㉓出差費用
㉔時差

㉑當地特產
㉒禮品

⑬schedule ⑭plant tour ⑮corporate brochure ⑯head office
⑰branch office ⑱sample ⑲network of connections ⑳local
cuisine ㉑local specialties ㉒gift ㉓travel expenses ㉔jet lag

1 我出差。
I go on a business trip.

2 我安排交通與住宿。
I make arrangements for travel and accommodation.

3 我請總務部安排我去上海出差的機票和住宿。
I ask the general affairs department to arrange the air tickets and accommodation for my business trip to Shanghai.

4 我為三天兩夜的出差做準備。
I prepare for a three-day, two-night business trip.

5 我製作出差時程表。
I make a schedule for my business trip.

tips

❷ accommodation 指「住宿」，而 make travel arrangements 就是「安排行程」。

❹「三天兩夜的出差」也可説成 a business trip of three days and two nights。

❺「行程表」也可用 timetable（時間表）。

6　我選定某人在我不在的時候代我處理事務。
I choose someone to be in charge while I'm away.

7　我租一台手機以便於國外出差時使用。
I rent a cellphone to use during my overseas business trip.

8　我順道拜訪分公司。
I drop by the branch office.

9　我去參觀工廠。
I go on a plant tour.

10　我進行店鋪查帳。
I conduct a store audit.

❻ be in charge 是「負責處理」之意，而 while I'm away 就是「當我不在的時候」。
❽ 此例句中的 drop by（順道拜訪）也可改為 visit（拜訪）。
❾ plant 指「工廠」。而此例句也可說成 I take a factory tour.。
❿ audit 是「審核；〔會計〕查帳」之意。而「進行現場調查」則說成 conduct an on-site investigation。

11 我為開設新的分公司而做準備。
I prepare to open a new branch [office].

12 我去視察最新的系統。
I go to inspect the latest system[s].

13 我和客戶互相問候。
I exchange greetings with the client.

14 我〔的出差行程〕被惡劣的天氣給耽誤了。
I am held up by the bad weather [on my business trip].

tips

⓫ branch office 是「分公司」，而「總公司；總部」則為 head office。

⓬ inspect 為「視察；檢查」之意，而「最新的」也可說成 newest。

⓭ 「打招呼」叫 greet，而「談生意」可說成 discuss a business matter。

⓯ 「請隨時通知我狀況」可說成 Please keep me posted.。

15 我與總公司聯絡。
I contact my head office.

16 我從出差地急忙趕回來。
I rush back from my business trip.

17 我替同部門的人買禮物。
I buy gifts for people in my section.

18 我先代墊了出差費用〔事後這些費用可以核銷〕。
I pay for my business travel expenses [which will be reimbursed later].

⑯「我從出差地趕回來而沒有過夜」可說成 I came back from my business trip quickly without staying overnight.。

⑰「給同部門的同事」也可說成 for my co-workers in my department。另外，若用 souvenir，則指「紀念品」。

⑱ reimburse 是「償還、核銷」之意。

1　這是我第一次到非英語系國家出差，我相當緊張。
It's my first business trip to a non-English-speaking country, so I'm rather nervous.

2　這可能是唯一在我們預算內的飯店。
This is probably the only hotel within our budget.

3　我們必須坐經濟艙去歐洲。現在我們公司的預算掐得非常緊。
We have to travel economy-class to Europe. Our company's budget control is very tight now.

4　我們現在比以前少出差了，因為經濟不景氣。
We don't have as many business trips as we used to because of the economic downturn.

5　這是個花八小時移動、參訪兩小時的當日來回出差行程。我一定會累壞的。
It's a one-day business trip with eight hours of traveling for a two-hour visit. I'll be totally worn out.

6　我必須好好規畫行程，這樣才能有效率地跑完所有地方。
I need to work out my schedule so that I can go around places without wasting time.

It's my first ~ = 這是我第一次的~／non-English-speaking country = 非英語系國家 cf. English-speaking countries = 英語系國家／rather nervous = 相當緊張

若不是「緊張」而是「滿心期待」，則可説成 I'm quite excited。

---

probably = 或許；可能／the only~ = 唯一的~／within budget = 在預算內

「超出預算」可説成 exceed the budget。

---

economy class (= coach) = 經濟艙 cf. first class = 頭等艙、business class = 商務艙／travel to ~ = 去~旅行／budget control = 預算管理／tight = 緊的；嚴格的

「我把我的機票從經濟艙升等到商務艙」可説成 I upgraded my ticket from economy class to business class.。

---

as many ~ as ... = 和…一樣多的~／used to ~ = 過去通常是~／economic downturn = 經濟不景氣

前半句直譯為中文就是「我們現在出差的次數不如以前多」。另外「經濟不景氣」也可用 sluggish economy、recession 等説法。

---

one-day = 單日的；當日來回的／traveling = 〔交通〕移動／totally = 完全地；徹底地／worn out = 筋疲力竭（worn 是 wear 的過去分詞）

「隔夜（住一晚）的旅行」叫 overnight trip。

---

work out ~ = 想出~；訂出~／go around ~ = 四處走動／without wasting time = 不浪費時間

「從一處移動到另一處」就説成 move from one place to another。

7 利用網路找去目的地最直接的路線真的很方便！

Finding the most direct route to the destination on the Internet is really convenient!

8 我會把我們的行程表和出差員工名單一起寄給他們。

I'll send them our schedule with the list of the employees who will go there.

9 我必須記得帶夠多的名片（企業宣傳小冊／樣品）去才行。

I have to remember to bring enough <u>business cards (corporate brochures/samples</u>).

10 我會把需要的資料全存進電腦裡，然後帶著電腦去。

I'll put all the data I need on my PC and bring it with me.

11 我們現在甚至可在火車上用網路。真方便！

We can even use the Internet on the train now. How convenient!

12 我會在去程的高鐵列車上將文件看過一遍。

I'll look through the document on the high-speed train on my way there.

find ~ on the Internet = 利用網路找~／the most direct route = 最直接的路線；最短路線／destination = 目的地

「在網上搜尋」可說成 search the Internet/Net。

---

send ~ with ... = 將~和⋯一起寄出／list = 名單；清單／employees who will go there = 將會去那邊的員工

若想強調「於事前」，則可把 beforehand 或 in advance 加在 our schedule 之後。

---

have to remenber to ~ = 必須記得做~／enough = 足夠的／business card = 名片／corporate = 企業的；公司的／brochure = 小冊子／sample = 樣品

「交換名片」說成 exchange business cards，而「可以給我一張名片嗎？」則說成 May I have your business card?。

---

put ~ on a PC = 把~存進電腦／bring ~ with me = 帶~和我一起去

筆記型電腦叫 laptop [computer]，或 notebook [computer]。而「在我的電腦裡安裝軟體」則說成 install software on my PC。

---

even = 甚至／use the Internet = 使用網路／How ~ ! = 真是~！／convenient = 方便的

「連上網路」說成 access/connect to the Internet，而「網路費」可用 Internet access fee。

---

look through ~ = 瀏覽~；查看~／document = 文件／high-speed train = 高速火車；高鐵列車／on my way ~ = 在我去~的路上

「在回程上」就說成 on the way back。

13 我很期待嚐嚐時令便當。

I'm looking forward to trying the seasonal lunch box.

14 我很緊張，因為我將一直和我老闆待在一起。我該不會要跟他同房吧？

I'm nervous because I'll be with my boss the whole time. I won't be sharing a room with him, will I?

15 我得要求電話叫醒服務（洗衣服務）。

I'll have to ask for a <u>wake-up call</u> (<u>laundry service</u>).

16 應該會有個人拿牌子來接我。

There is supposed to be someone with a sign to pick me up.

17 李先生本人似乎比他的電子郵件來得友善得多。

Mr. Lee seems much nicer in person than through e-mail.

18 和某人面對面講過話，而不只是藉由電話與電子郵件聯絡，之後和他們合作起來就會更輕鬆。

When you've spoken to someone face-to-face instead of just contacting via phone and e-mail, you can work with them much more easily.

look forward to ~ = 期待~（to 後面若遇動詞要用 ing 形式）／try = 嘗試／
seasonal = 時令的；當季的 cf. season = 季節／lunch box = 便當
「火車便當」可說成 a boxed <u>meal</u>/<u>lunch</u> sold on the train。

nervous = 緊張的／the whole time = 自始至終；一直／share a room = 共住
一間房／I won't be ~, will I? = 我該不會要~吧？（won't = will not）
「住飯店」可說成 stay at a hotel，而「單人房」則叫 single room。

ask for ~ = 要求~；請求~／a wake-up call = 電話叫醒服務／laundry = 洗
衣 cf. dry cleaning = 乾洗
「麻煩，我想要 7 點的電話叫醒服務」說成 I'd like a wake-up call at 7:00,
please.。

supposed to be ~ = 應該~；理當~／sign = 招牌；標誌 cf. signboard = 告
示牌／pick ~ up = 接~（人）
本例句也可說成 There should be someone with a sign to pick me up.。

much nicer = 友善得多／in person = 親自／through ~ = 透過~
「與本人親自會面」可說成 meet in person。而「我對~的第一印象」則可用
my first impression of ~ 表達。

face-to-face = 面對面 e.g. face-to-face talk = 面對面談話／instead of ~
= 而不是~；代替~／contact = 聯絡／via ~ = 經由~；藉~／much more
easily = 容易得多
「請用電話或電子郵件與我聯絡」可說成 Please contact me by phone or
e-mail.。

19 能見到關鍵人物真的很有幫助。
It was useful to meet the key person.

20 我的出差行程因對方的問題而突然取消。
My business trip was suddenly canceled because of a problem on the other side.

21 我們現在有辦法聯絡上正在國外出差的經理嗎？
Can we get in contact with the manager who is on an overseas business trip right now?

22 我既然花了公司的差旅費大老遠地跑到這兒來，就必須做出點成果。
I have to produce some results, since I came all the way here using company travel expenses.

23 我們盡力談妥了一筆生意。大老遠跑來總算是值得了。
We managed to close a deal. It was worth coming all the way here.

24 到場親眼看過該處和只是看看書面資料，真的是很不一樣的。
Seeing the actual place with your own eyes is really different from just looking at the documents.

useful = 有益的；有用的／key person = 關鍵人物

注意，key person 是指「關鍵人物」，但不一定是「承辦人」、「負責人」。「承辦人」、「負責人」要說成 the person in charge。

---

be canceled = 取消／the other side = 另一方（對方）

「我的出差行程在最後一刻被取消」可說成 My business trip was canceled at the last minute.。

---

get in contact with ~ = 與～取得聯繫／be on an overseas business trip = 正在國外出差／right now = 現在；此刻

「我聯絡不上他」說成 I can't <u>reach</u>/<u>get hold of</u> him.。

---

produce = 做出／result = 結果；成果／all the way = 大老遠地／travel expenses = 差旅費

「我們一無所獲」可說成 We came up empty-handed.。

---

manage to ~ = 設法做到～／close a deal = 成交一筆生意／worth ~ing = 值得做～

「這一趟相當值得」可說成 The trip was well worth it.。

---

see ~ with one's own eyes = 用自己的眼睛看～；親眼目睹～／actual = 實際的／document = 文件；資料

「百聞不如一見」說成 Seeing is believing.。

25 此行的最佳收穫就是能到我平常沒機會去的當地商店看看。
The best part of my trip was being able to go to the local shops that I don't usually have the chance to see.

26 不管怎樣，這次雖然只建立了人脈，也算不錯了。
Anyway, I will have to settle for having built up a network of connections.

27 我要快快完成這工作，這樣我就能出去找點樂子了！
I will get this work done quickly so that I can go out and have some fun!

28 我的行程太緊湊了！根本沒時間觀光。
My schedule is too tight! I have no time for sightseeing.

29 無論我出差到哪裡，我都非常喜歡品嚐當地的美食。
I always enjoy eating local food wherever my trip takes me to.

30 我弄丟了一些收據，不知道這樣是否還能報帳。
I've lost some receipts, and I wonder if I can get my travel expenses paid back.

the best part of ~ = ~最棒的部分／local = 當地的／have the chance to ~ = 有機會做~

「地方色彩」叫 local color，「當地特產」則叫 local specialty。

---

anyway = 無論如何；不管怎樣／settle for ~ = 勉強接受~／have built up = 建立了（built 是 build 的過去式和過去分詞）／a network of connections = 人脈（connection = 連結；關係）

「建立工作上的人際網路（交流、人脈）」叫 networking。

---

get ~ done = 把~完成／so that ~ = 以便~／go out = 出去／have fun = 享樂；玩耍

「今天的工作已完成」可說成 We're done for today. 或 That does it for today.。而「今天就做到這裡為止吧！」則說成 Let's call it a day!。

---

tight = 緊湊的／have no time for ~ = 沒時間做~／sightseeing = 觀光；旅遊

「進行觀光導覽」可說成 do sightseeing!。

---

enjoy = 享受（其後若遇到動詞時應用 ing 形式）／local food = 當地食物／wherever = 無論在何處

想問「這裡的特色菜是什麼？」可說成 What is the specialty here?。

I've lost = 我弄丟了（lost 為 lose 的過去式和過去分詞）／receipt = 收據／I wonder if ~ = 不知是否能~／pay back = 償還 cf. reimburse = 報銷

「麻煩請給我收據」說成 I would like a receipt, please.，而「我必須留存所有收據」則可說成 I have to keep all my receipts.。

31 雖然我不覺得有必要大老遠來這兒出差，但是吃到了一些美食，所以就還好。

I don't think I needed to come all the way here on a business trip, but I had some delicious food, so it was OK.

32 下次我想來這邊純粹旅遊。

I'd like to come here just to travel for pleasure next time.

33 我的時差一直調不回來。

I can't get over this jet lag.

need to ～ = 有必要做～／delicious food = 好吃的食物

「這真好吃！」可説成 It's <u>delicious</u>/<u>tasty</u>! 或 It tastes good!。

I'd like to ～ = 我想做～（I'd = I would）／travel for pleasure = 旅遊 cf. travel for business = 出差

此例句也可説成 I'd like to come here just for sightseeing next time.「下次我想來此觀光」。

---

get over ～ = 恢復～；克服～／jet lag = （跨時區飛行後的）生理時差

注意，「各地的時間差異（時差）」應説成 time difference。另，「我因時差而生體不適」可説成 I'm jet-lagged.。

基本的商務電子郵件寫法

　　在網際網路如此發達的今日，比起實際和對方面對面以英語談生意，透過電子郵件進行商品下單及交易等的機會其實更多。電子郵件不像會話那樣可以當場改口，故其內容必須更嚴謹才行。在此，為讀者介紹英文商務電子郵件的撰寫訣竅。

一. 商務電子郵件禮儀

　　撰寫商務電子郵件和撰寫給朋友的郵件不同。為了能確實充分傳達自己要說的事情，請務必注意以下幾點。
- 須依定型化格式來寫（請參考下面「商務電子郵件的結構」部分）。
- 務必使用簡潔易懂的句子。
- 避免使用抽象的表達方式。
- 日期、時間、數值等都應明確寫入。

二. 商務電子郵件的結構

　　只要依據以下模式來撰寫，便能夠更確實地傳達自己要說的事情。

1. Subject line（主旨）
為了能吸引對方注意，請將欲傳達之事簡潔地摘要成主旨。
e.g. Inquiry about ...（有關…的疑問）／Request for ...（請求…）
　　 Quotation for ...（…的報價）／Confirmation of ...（確認…）

2. Greeting（問候）
依據對方身分及信件內容正式程度之不同，開頭可使用 Dear 或 Hello。
e.g. Dear Sir or Madam（親愛的先生或女士）＊用於不知對方姓名的情況下
　　 Hello, Mr. Johnson（強森先生，您好）＊較普通的稱呼方式

3. Body（內文）
以如下的段落結構為基礎，撰寫簡潔的內文。
❶起頭（應明確敘述撰寫此信的目的，以及希望對方回覆些什麼）

e.g. I'm writing to ...（我之所以寫信來，是為了…）

This is in response to ...（此信是為了回應…）

❷具體事由（若是提案、下單等，就單刀直入；若是要拒絕或道歉，則用字遣詞就需小心謹慎）

e.g. Would you please send ...?（能否請您寄送…過來？）

I'm very sorry to inform you ...（很抱歉我必須通知您…）

❸結尾（以確認、道歉、感謝、期待等固定句子作結）

e.g. We would appreciate it if you could ...（若您能…我們將非常感激）

I look forward to -ing ...（我很期待…）

4. Closing line（信末敬詞）

請依對方身分及信件的正式程度來選擇信末敬詞。若是同一對象，那麼每次都該使用相同的敬詞。

e.g. Sincerely yours、Yours sincerely＊用於正式信件，屬於嚴謹的敬詞

Best regards、Best wishes＊較普通的敬詞

5. Signature（署名）

依序寫上姓名、職務、部門、公司名稱（含聯絡資訊）。這部分可事先製作並登錄好，以便使用。

e.g. Alex Chu（姓名）

Assistant Manager（職務）

Marketing Department（部門名稱）

Taiwan Tele-Net Trading, Co.（公司名稱）

撰寫英文商務電子郵件時，不能期待對方能體諒這是非英語母語者所寫的。縱使詞句和語氣都很難寫到完美，但仍應時時注意是否有錯字、漏字，盡可能寫出正確的文句。

Skit  出差篇

南美出差行，已準備就緒，鬥志超高昂

Woman: **The boss asked me to go on a business trip to Venezuela❶.**

Man: **Wow, that's great!**

W: **Well, I have to make arrangements for travel and accommodation myself.**

M: **Oh, too bad.**

W: **No, finding the route on the Internet is really convenient.**

M: **Oh, that's good. What does he want you to do there?**

W: **I have to take a factory tour, conduct a store audit and prepare to open a new branch.**

M: **Oh, you'll have to take a lot of documents❷.**

W: **No. I'll put all the data I need on my PC and take it with me.**

M: **You'll enjoy it. It's a beautiful country.**

W: **But my schedule will be too tight. I won't have any time for sightseeing.**

M: **You'd better❸ buy some gifts for the people in this section.**

W: **Yes. The best part will be going to local shops you wouldn't be able to see anywhere else.**

女子：老闆要我去委內瑞拉出差。

男子：哇，真棒！

女：嗯，我必須自己安排交通與住宿。

男：噢，那就累人了。

女：不會，利用網路找出路線真的很方便！

男：喔，那就好。老闆叫妳去那裡要做什麼？

女：我必須參觀工廠、進行店鋪查帳，並為開設新分公司而做準備。

男：喔，那妳得帶很多文件吧。

女：並不需要。我會把需要的資料全存進電腦裡，然後帶著電腦去。

男：妳會玩得很開心的。那是個很美的國家。

女：可是我的行程太緊湊了。根本不會有時間觀光。

男：妳最好替這個部門的人買點禮物。

女：我會的。此行的最佳收穫將是能到別處看不到的當地商店逛逛。

【單字片語】

❶ Venezuela：委內瑞拉

❷ document：文件

❸ you'd better ~：你最好～

Quick Check

讓我們一起來複習本章所介紹過的句型！請依據以下中文句子的意思，完成對應的英文句子。（答案就在本頁最下方）

❶ 我順道拜訪分公司。 →P103
I ( ) ( ) the ( ) ( ).

❷ 我〔的出差行程〕被惡劣的天氣給耽誤了。 →P104
I am ( ) ( ) by the bad weather [on my business trip].

❸ 這可能是唯一在我們預算內的飯店。 →P106
This is probably the ( ) hotel ( ) ( ) ( ).

❹ 這是個花八小時移動、參訪兩小時的當日來回出差行程。我一定會累壞的。 →P106
It's a ( ) ( ) ( ) with eight hours of traveling for a two-hour visit. I'll be totally ( ) ( ).

❺ 我得要求電話叫醒服務。 →P110
I'll have to ask for a ( ) ( ).

❻ 應該會有個人拿牌子來接我。 →P110
There is supposed to be someone with a ( ) to ( ) me ( ).

❼ 能見到關鍵人物真的很有幫助。 →P112
It was ( ) to meet the ( ) ( ).

❽ 我們盡力談妥了一筆生意。大老遠跑來總算值得了。 →P112
We ( ) to ( ) ( ) ( ). It was ( ) coming ( ) ( ) ( ) here.

❾ 此行的最佳收穫就是能到我平常沒機會去的當地商店看看。 →P114
The ( ) ( ) ( ) my trip was being able to go to the local shops that I don't usually ( ) ( ) ( ) to see.

❿ 我的時差一直調不回來。 →P116
I can't ( ) ( ) this ( ) ( ).

---

❶drop/by/branch/office ❷held/up ❸only/within/our/budget ❹one-day/business/trip/worn/out ❺wake-up/call ❻sign/pick/up ❼useful/key/person ❽managed/close/a/deal/worth/all/the/way ❾best/part/of/have/the/chance ❿get/over/jet/lag

chapter 5

企劃、開發
Planning & Development

 工作量超大、
腦袋又得動個不停,
就屬企劃、開發類工作了。
從市場調查中尋找創意,
再實際商品化,
並安排廣告宣傳,
本章便要為你介紹這一連串的流程。

Words 單字篇

❼競爭對手

❶市場調查

❸目標對象
❹潛在顧客

❽趨勢

❺需求
❻利基

❷問卷

NEW!

❾網路廣告

❿終端用戶；最終消費者
⓫售後服務
⓬口碑

❶marketing research ❷questionnaire ❸target ❹prospective customers ❺need ❻niche ❼competitor ❽trend ❾web advertisement ❿end user ⓫after-sales service ⓬word of mouth ⓭draft proposal ⓮budget ⓯cost-benefit performance ⓰project

首先，讓我們透過各種事、物的名稱，
來掌握「企劃、開發」工作給人的整體印象。

⑭預算
⑮成本效益
⑬企劃草案
⑯專案
⑰商品開發
⑱規格
⑲主要商品
⑳仿冒品
㉑競爭；競賽
㉒促銷
㉓媒體發表會
㉔活動
㉕新聞稿

⑰product development ⑱specifications ⑲staple item
⑳knockoff ㉑competition ㉒sales promotion ㉓press event
㉔campaign ㉕press release

1 我們研究客戶需求。
We do research on the needs of our clients.

2 我們做市場調查。
We do marketing research.

3 我們實施問卷調查。
We do a questionnaire survey.

4 我們縮小目標市場。
We narrow down the target market.

5 我詢問身邊人們的意見。
I ask people close to me for their opinions.

tips

❶「配合～的需求」應說成 <u>meet</u>/<u>suit</u> one's needs。
❷「總結調查結果」就說成 round up the results of the research。
❸「統計問卷調查結果」可說成 summarize the questionnaire results。另外請注意，questionnaire 的發音為 [kwɛstʃən`ɛr]。
❹「符合目標市場」就說成 fit the target market。

6 我們對準市場利基。
We target a market niche.

7 我們研究競爭對手的動向。
We study the moves of our competitors.

8 我去到競爭對手的店裡。
I go into a competitor's shop.

9 我去市內調查最近的趨勢。
I go to the city to check out the recent trends.

10 我讓我的企劃通過審核。
I get my plan approved.

❻ niche 是指「利基；優勢」，e.g. niche business（利基型產業）。
❼ competitor（競爭對手）也可用 rival（敵手）來表示。
❿ 「執行企劃案」可說成 go on with a plan。

11 我們進行腦力激盪。
We do brainstorming.

12 我們開發一項產品。
We develop a product.

13 我們考量各個層面以設定價格。
We set prices, taking various aspects into account.

14 我們面臨激烈競爭。
We are faced with fierce competition.

15 我擬出企劃草案〔以做進一步討論〕。
I draw up a draft proposal [for further discussion].

tips

⓫ brainstorm 若做為名詞使用，也有「靈機一動；突發奇想」之類的意思，e.g. have a brainstorm（想到一個好點子）。

⓭ set the price <u>high</u> (<u>low</u>) 則是「將價格定得高（低）」。

⓮ be faced with...指「面臨…」。而 fierce 則為「激烈的」之意。

⓯「企劃草案」還有 strawman proposal 這種講法可用。

16 我們縮減構想數量，只留下幾個最好的。
We narrow down our ideas to a few of the best ones.

17 我們重新設計我們的主要商品。
We redesign our staple items.

18 我們展開了新商品的開發。
We launch the development of a new product.

19 我們有了突破性的創新。
We come up with a breakthrough innovation.

20 我估算成本效益。
I <u>calculate</u>/<u>assess</u> the cost-benefit performance.

---

⑰ 英語的 renew 是「更新〔期限等〕」的意思，並不用來表示商品的「更新」。另外「主要商品」也可用 regular <u>items/goods</u>。

⑱ 「展開～」也可用 embark on ～ 來表達。

⑲ come up with 就是「想出〔新創意〕」之意。

21 我草擬一個預算企劃。
I draw up a budget proposal.

22 我們維持不超出預算。
We keep it within budget.

23 我們開始一個新專案。
We start a new project.

24 我訂出進度表。
I work out a schedule.

25 我們重新安排進度。
We rearrange our schedule.

tips

㉑ 「分配預算」就說成 allocate a budget。

㉒ 「我們的預算很緊」可說成 We are on a tight budget.。

㉔ 此例句也可用 map（詳細計畫）這個動詞，說成 I map out a schedule.。

㉕ 若要使用 reschedule（重新安排）這個字，後面就必須接上變更的東西，e.g. reschedule the meeting（重新安排會議時間）。

26 我擬定規格。
I draw up specifications.

27 我向我老闆報告專案進度。
I report the progress of the project to my boss.

28 我們測試產品品質。
We test the quality of the product.

29 我們將工作外包出去。
We outsource jobs.

30 我們與相關部門協調。
We coordinate with the departments concerned.

㉗ 「那個企劃案的進度如何了？」可説成 What's the progress on the proposal? 或者 How's the proposal coming along?。

㉙ 「將～外包給…」可説成 <u>outsource</u>/<u>contract out</u> ~ to ...。

㉚ 「協調者的角色」可用 coordinating role 表示，e.g. The manager played a coordinating role this time.（這次由經理扮演協調的角色）。

31 我們在自己的網站上刊登一則廣告。
We place an advertisement on our website.

32 我建立一個促銷計畫。
I create a plan for promoting sales.

33 我們與另一家公司合作。
We collaborate with another company.

34 我們舉辦新產品的媒體發表會。
We hold a press event to launch a new product.

35 我發出新聞稿給各媒體。
I send out a press release to the media.

tips

㉛ 「刊登廣告」也可說成 run an advertisement。

㉝ produce ~ in collaboration with ... 可表達「與⋯合作生產～」之意。

㉞ press event 是指「針對媒體舉辦的活動、發表會」。

㉟ 「〔商品的〕銷售通路」也可說成 sales outlet。

36 我們開發一個銷售通路。
We develop a distribution channel.

37 我們選定廣告媒體。
We choose advertising media.

38 我們測量廣告效果。
We measure advertising effectiveness.

39 我們結合產品上市，舉辦一場活動。
We kick off a campaign in conjunction with the product launch.

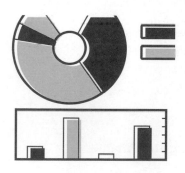

40 我找了幾家廣告代理商來競價。
I ask for competitive bids/estimates from several ad agencies.

㊲ 「平面媒體廣告」說成 print advertisement，「電子媒體廣告」則是 electronic advertisement。

㊴ kick off 除了用於足球賽外，也經常用來表達「〔活動等〕開始進行」的意思。而 in conjunction with ~ 就是「結合～」之意。

㊵ 「競價；競標」也可只用 bids 或 estimates。

1 市場上的競爭真的很激烈。
There really is a rat race going on in the market.

2 現在的終端使用者太聰明了，不會輕易被大企業操縱。
End users these days are too smart to be manipulated easily by big businesses.

3 讓我們忘掉之前所有的成功經驗。
Let's forget all the successful experiences we've had before now.

4 最好能夠深入思考使用者的需求。
It's better to reflect the needs of the users.

5 這產品的目標對象到底是誰啊？
Who the hell is this product targeted at?

6 我們必須將老年人市場納入考量。
We have to take the senior market into account.

rat race = 嚴酷的生存競爭／go on = 繼續進行

rat race 是由老鼠的行為（重複同樣的動作，只會累垮，其餘一無所獲）所衍伸而來的講法。「激烈的競爭」也可用 scramble 來表達，e.g. There's a mad scramble in the cellphone market.（手機市場有著瘋狂的激烈競爭）。

---

end user = 終端用戶；最終消費者／too ~ to ... = 太過~以至於無法…／be manipulated = 被操縱／big business = 大企業

「玩弄~；戲弄~」可說成 play cat and mouse with ~，e.g. Big businesses sometimes seem to be playing cat and mouse with customers.（大企業有時像是在玩弄顧客）。

---

forget = 忘記；捨棄／successful = 成功的

「回歸根本」就說成 go back to basics，e.g. Let's go back to basics and look at the project with a fresh eye.（讓我們回歸根本，以全新眼光重新審視此專案）。

It's better to ~ = 最好~／reflect = 深思；反省

「設身處地為人著想」可用 put oneself in someone's shoes 來表達，e.g. You have to put yourself in the customers' shoes.（你必須站在顧客的立場替顧客著想）。

Who the hell ~? = 到底誰是~？（相當口語化的講法）

服務或活動等「以~為對象」可用 be intended for ~ 來表示，e.g. This PC workshop is intended for beginners who need typing skills.（這個電腦研習營以需要學會打字技術的初學者為對象）。

---

take ~ into account = 將~納入考量

也可利用動詞 eye 來表達納入考量之意，如 eye the senior market。另外「拓展、擴大市場」可說成 expand/enlarge the market。

7　讓我們把從家庭主婦那邊收集到的真實意見好好地運用於商品開發。

Let's make good use of the real <u>voices</u>/<u>opinions</u> collected from housewives for product development.

8　那是舊資料。難道我們沒有最新資料嗎？

That is the old data. Don't we have the latest data?

9　有時我實在搞不懂，到底是什麼吸引了顧客。

Sometimes I have no idea what gets the customer hooked.

10　太棒了！我們的銷量和收益都已贏過去年。

Great! We've gained more sales and earnings than last year.

11　喔，這點子不錯。我要據為己有。

Oh, that's a good idea. I'm going to call it mine.

12　基本上，隨意想到的點子往往都無法實現。

Basically, random ideas often end up going up in smoke.

make good use of ～ = 妥善利用～／product development = 商品開發

「將創意發展成新產品」可説成 develop the idea into a new product。而「進行與商品有關的問卷調查」則可説成 do/conduct a questionnaire survey on the product。

Don't we ～ =〔難道我們〕沒有～？／latest = 最新的

latest 為 late（最近的）的最高級。而「更新過的資料」説成 updated data；「修正過的資料」説成 revised data；「銷毀資料」則説成 destroy data，e.g. Please destroy the data after reading it.（資料讀完後請銷毀）。

get ～ hooked = 使～著迷；讓～被吸引

「我們永遠不知道什麼東西會暢銷」可説成 We never know what will be in.，其中的 in 做為形容詞使用，為「流行的；受歡迎的」之意。

gain = 獲得／earnings = 收益（用複數）

「與去年／前一年相比」可説成 compared to last year/the previous year，e.g. Our income has grown 5 percent compared to last year/the previous year.（與去年／前一年相比，我們公司的收益已成長了百分之五）。

call ～ mine = 把～説成是自己的東西

mine 為「所有代名詞」，在此代替 my idea。

basically = 基本上／random = 隨意的；隨機的／end up ～ing = 終究會～／go up in smoke = 灰飛煙滅；化為烏有

「隨便想到」也可用 off the top of one's head 這種講法來表達，e.g. The idea is just off the top of my head.（那只是我隨便想到的點子）。

13 我知道你的點子極具獨創性，但是就現今而言它似乎有些脫離現實。

I know how original your idea is but it seems a bit too far out for the current times.

14 我必須說，你的點子聽來十分獨特，但是不切實際。

I must say your idea sounds unique, but far-fetched.

15 你的提案也許不好，但使用 PowerPoint 至少能使它看起來好。

Your proposal may not *be* good, but at least, with PowerPoint you can make it *look* good.

16 她的企劃看起來更有吸引力。

Her proposal looks more attractive.

17 我的企劃案又被否決了。已經四連敗了。

I got my proposal turned down again. This is the fourth time in a row.

18 首先我們該決定，是要創造需求還是搶攻市場。

We should start off by deciding whether we'll create need or grab market share.

original = 有獨創性的／far out = 脫離現實／current times = 現今

「走在時代前端」可說成 be ahead of the times，e.g. The fuel supply system is ahead of the times. (這種燃料供給系統走在時代前端)。

I must say ~ = 我必須說~／far-fetched = 牽強的

far-fetched 的 "fetch" 是「去拿過來」的意思，故 far-fetched 字面上是「從遠處拿過來的」，轉指「牽強的」之意。在此可用 unrealistic (不切實際的) 來代替。

---

at least = 至少

---

attractive = 有魅力的；有吸引力的

本句的 attractive 可用 appealing (吸引人的) 代替。

---

get ~ turned down = ~被否決／in a row = 連續；一連

「拒絕、否決」也可使用 reject 這個字，說成 get ~ rejected。而「獲得採用」則用 adopt，e.g. Finally, my proposal got adopted. (我的企劃案終於被採用了)。

---

start off by ~ing = 從做~開始／whether ~ = 是否要~／grab = 獲取；搶奪

英文的 pie (派) 可用來指「整體；總額」的意思，e.g. Axcellor Inc. takes a big share of the online advertising pie. (艾克斯勒公司在整個線上廣告市場中佔有很大的比例)。

19 我們無法光靠一個點子來進行這個計畫。

We can't go on with this plan with just a single idea.

20 這個構想對我們的贊助商來說應該很有吸引力。

That idea should sound appealing to our sponsors.

21 我們應該提供更好的售後服務，以促進顧客回流。

We should provide better after-sale service to encourage return customers.

22 在構思新點子方面我遇上了瓶頸。

I'm stuck in a rut when it comes to getting new ideas.

23 我很好奇怎樣的車能夠感動女人心。

I wonder what type of car stirs women's emotions.

24 你知道的，一個老（男）人能想出的東西是有限的。

You know there's a limit to what an old man can think of.

go on with ~ = 開始做~／single = 單一的

plan 除指一般的「計畫」之外，也可用來表示「方案」，e.g. a good corporate plan （一個好的公司方案）。

---

appealing = 吸引人的 cf. appeal to = 吸引／sponsor = 贊助商

be received well by ~ 也有「深受~歡迎」之意，e.g. His presentation was received well by the board.（他的簡報深受董事會的喜愛）。

---

after-sale service = 售後服務／encourage = 促進；鼓勵／return customer = 回流的顧客

「重要的顧客」可說成 valued customer。

---

be stuck in a rut = 陷入一成不變的狀態（遇上瓶頸無法突破）／when it comes to ~ = 談到~時

「〔生活、工作是〕單調的；一成不變的」可用 humdrum 來形容，e.g. I got bored with the humdrum nine-to-five routine.（我厭倦了朝九晚五的單調工作）

---

stir = 刺激；撥動／emotion = 情感

「女人心」也可說成 woman's feelings/mind，e.g. You don't understand women's feelings.（你真是不懂女人心）、A woman's mind and a winter wind change oft.（＜俗語＞女人心如冬天的風，說變就變）。

You know = 你知道的／old man = 老（男）人

欲嘲諷一個人「腦袋不靈活、保守」時，也可用 stick in the mud 來表達，例如 My boss is such a stick in the mud.（我老闆真是個老頑固）。

25 我從沒想出什麼好點子。我應該更常出門去找點靈感。
I never get any good ideas. I should go out more often and get some inspiration.

26 嘿，這不是仿冒我們產品的盜版貨嗎？
Hey, isn't this a knockoff of our product?

27 可惡！鎂諾克斯公司的新產品搶先了我們一步。
Darn! The recent product of Magnox is just one step ahead of us.

28 如果我們繼續努力，這點子有可能成為一個了不起的案子。
This idea could turn out to be something if we keep working on it.

29 除非我們能製造出大受歡迎的東西，否則這部門就沒未來了。
The department has no future unless we produce a hit right now.

30 我對這個專案有著特殊的情感，因為我從規劃階段就開始參與了。
I have a special attachment to the project because I've been working on it since the planning stage.

inspiration = 激勵;靈感

「想出點子」可説成 come up with an idea,而「擠出構想」則説成 squeeze out an idea。另外「出去轉換心情」可説成 go outside for a change。

---

knockoff = 仿冒品;山寨版

「偽造;仿造」可用 counterfeit 表示,e.g. They counterfeit our products. (他們仿製我們的產品)。

Darn = 可惡;該死/one step ahead of ~ = 搶先~一步

其它有用到 one step(一步)的常見句型還有 We are left one step behind. (我們落後了一步)、You can do it one step at a time.(你可以一步步慢慢地做)。

---

turn out to be ~ = 結果成為~/something = 了不起的事物/work on ~ = 努力處理~

something 也可用來指人,e.g. The new boss is really something.(新來的主管真的是個了不起的人物)。

---

unless ~ = 除非~/hit = 受歡迎的事物

「陷入絕境」可説成 be driven into a ditch 或 have one's back against the wall,e.g. Due to the cancellation of the big project, we had our backs against the wall.(由於大案子被取消,我們陷入了絕境)。

---

special attachment to ~ = 對~的特殊情感/planning stage = 規劃階段

「對~有著很深的感情」可説成 be deeply attached to~;e.g. I'm deeply attached to this department.(我對這個部門有著很深的感情)。

31 如果沒能參加上明天的比賽，我所有的努力就都將付諸流水。
All my efforts will go right down the drain if I can't make it to the competition tomorrow.

32 我要研究上次比賽敗陣的原因，這樣下次我才不會再輸。
I'm going to study why I lost in the last competition so I won't lose in the next one.

33 這個計畫一定能通過的。
This plan is sure to get the green light.

34 從我進這間公司開始，我就一直夢想著這個企劃案能通過。
It's been my dream to get this proposal approved since I joined the company.

35 希望將來有一天，我能執行一個百萬美元的專案。
I wish I could run a million-dollar project some time in the future.

36 價格競爭越來越激烈。
Price competition is getting severe.

go down the drain = 成為泡影／make it to ~ = 參加~／competition = 競爭；競賽

make it 可用來指「成功」，e.g. He finally made it.（他終於成功了）；make it 也可用來指「趕上」，e.g. We made it in time for her wedding.（我們及時趕上她的婚禮）。

---

study = 研究／lose = 輸（lost 為過去式和過去分詞）

「為了不~」也可用 so as not to ~、in order not to ~ 等説法表達，e.g. He worded hard <u>so as not to</u>/<u>in order not to</u> fail again.（為了避免再次失敗，他努力地工作）。

---

get the green light = 獲得許可

「獲准繼續進行」也可説成 get the go-ahead。而「被斷然否決」則説成 get shot down，e.g. My proposal got shot down in the first stage.（我的企劃案在第一階段就被否決了）。

---

get ~ approved = 使~獲得認可／join the company = 進公司

join 一般指「參加；加入」，e.g. Would you like to join us?（你要不要加入我們的行列？）。

I wish I could ~ = 我希望我能~；要是我可以~就好了／run = 經營；管理／some time in the future = 將來有一天

注意，run 的特殊用法還包括「刊登〔廣告〕」，e.g. We're going to run an ad in the newspaper.（我們將在報紙上登廣告）。

---

price competition (= price war) = 價格競爭／severe = 嚴重的；劇烈的

「具有價格競爭力的產品」可説成 competitively-priced product，e.g. Generally, customers want a high-quality but competitively-priced product.（一般來説，顧客都想要高品質但具價格競爭力的產品）。

37 成本那麼高，我不覺得我們有辦法說服那些主管們進行這項計畫。
I doubt we can convince the executives to go ahead with this plan when the costs are that high.

---

38 這表示我們賣越多，就會虧越多。
That means the more we sell, the more of a deficit we'll be suffering from.

---

39 想到預算這麼少，我的創意也不禁變得貧乏。
With such a small budget in mind, I can't help running low on ideas.

---

40 業務員想說什麼就說什麼，但是他們根本不知道要將構想實現有多麼地困難。
Sales staff say whatever they want, but they don't realize how hard it is to implement an idea.

---

41 我對品質有百分之百的信心，但是談到設計，我不知該說些什麼。
I'm 100 percent sure of the quality, but I don't know what to say when it comes to the design.

---

42 沒錯，品質很重要，但是如果趕不上期限，就沒有任何意義。
True, quality is important, but it doesn't mean a thing if you can't meet the deadline.

I doubt ～ = 我懷疑～／convince ～ to ... = 說服～做…／executive = 主管／
go ahead with ～ = 進行～

win ~ over 也是經常用來表達「說服～」之意的說法，e.g. I wonder if I can
win my boss over to give me a raise.（不知我能否說服老闆幫我加薪）。

---

that means ～ = 這意味著～／the more ～, the more ... = 越～就越…／
deficit = 虧損／suffer from ～ = 承受～之苦

「有赤字；有虧損」可說成 in the red，e.g. The company keeps running in
the red.（這間公司持續虧損中）。另，「有盈餘」則說成 in the black，e.g.
We finally manage to stay in the black this year.（今年我們終於有了盈餘）。

---

with ～ in mind = 心裡想著～／can't help ～ing = 不禁～／run low on ～ = ～
低落；～變得貧乏

反之，若是靈感湧現，便可用 turn on the light bulb（點亮燈炮；靈機一動）
這種說法，e.g. A brief talk with an engineer turned on the light bulb in my
mind.（與工程師的一番簡短談話令我靈機一動）。

---

whatever they want [to say] = 一切他們所想〔說〕的／implement = 執
行～；實施～

「可實現的；可行的」除了能用 realize（實現）的形容詞 realizable 來表達
外，也可用 feasible，e.g. a feasible plan（一項可行的計畫）

---

be 100 percent sure of ～ = 百分之百確定～／when it comes to ～ = 當談到～

對重要的事情「含糊其辭」可用 dodge the subject 來表達，e.g. My
supervisor dodges the subject when it comes to my job advancement.（談到
關於我工作升遷的話題時，我的上司就開始含糊其辭）。

---

not mean a thing = 一點意義也沒有／meet the deadline = 趕上最後期限

「～到期的」可用 due 這個字，e.g. The report is due [on] next Monday.（這
份報告下週一到期）。

43 他們怎麼會期望我在三個月內完成這項工作？這是不可能的。

How come they expect me to get this done in three months? It's impossible.

44 你知道的，最重要的是團隊精神。

What counts most is teamwork, you know.

45 我想我又必須徹夜工作了。

I guess I'm going to have to work through the night again.

46 要是我們能有更多的促銷預算就好了。

If only we could have a bigger budget for sales promotion.

47 我們應該將使用者的觀點納入考量，並想出一句能深植人心的口號。

We should take the users' perspectives into account and come up with a slogan that sticks in their minds.

48 我相信在時裝雜誌上登廣告，對潛在顧客是有效的。

I believe placing an ad in fashion magazines will be effective for the prospective customers.

How come ~? = 怎麼會～？（含有責怪的語氣）／expect ~ to ... = 期望～
做…／get ~ done = 完成～；做到～

「超出某人的能力範圍」可用 beyond one's power 來表達，e.g. Getting this
done in three months is beyond my power.（三個月內完成是超出我能力範圍
的事）。

what counts is ~ = 重要的是～／you know = 你知道的

此例句也可說成 Teamwork is everything.（團隊精神就是一切）或 Teamwork
is what it takes to win.（想贏，就必須有團隊精神）。

I guess ~ = 我想／through the night = 徹夜

「徹夜」還有 pull an all-nighter 這種說法可用，e.g. I pulled an all-nighter
yesterday and finished the quarterly report.（我昨天徹夜完成了季報告書）。

if only ~ = 要是～的話就好了／sales promotion = 促銷／budget = 預算

be on a tight budget 就是「預算吃緊」，e.g. We can't afford to hire new staff
because we are on a tight budget.（我們雇不起新人，因為我們預算吃緊）。

take ~ into account = 將～納入考量／perspective = 看法；觀點／come up
with ~ = 想出～／slogan = 口號；標語；廣告詞／stick in ~ = 一直留存在～

「有能夠吸引人的東西」可用 have a good hook 來表達，e.g. We need a
background story that has a good hook.（我們需要一個能吸引人的背景故
事）。

place an ad = 刊登廣告／fashion magazine = 時裝雜誌／effective = 有效的
／prospective customer = 潛在顧客

prospective 的原名詞 prospect 也經常以「潛在顧客；預期客戶」之意被運
用，e.g. We expect that millions of target prospects will visit our website.（我
們預計會有數百萬個潛在顧客來參觀我們的網站）。

49 你覺得在發行量最大的報紙上刊登廣告如何？

What do you say to running an ad in the largest circulating paper?

50 如果使用不當，網站可能會對銷售造成負面影響。

The website can have a negative effect on sales if you don't use it properly.

51 我不知道該做什麼才能提高我們橫幅廣告的點閱率。

I wonder what I should do to raise the click-rate of our banner ad.

52 不管怎麼說，電視的影響力都不可小覷。

No matter what you say, you can't underestimate the impact TV has.

53 口碑肯定能創造奇蹟。

Word of mouth definitely works wonders.

run an ad = 打廣告／circulating = 流通的

What do you say to ~ing? 這種句型可用來探詢對方意見，或邀請對方。若取前者的意思，就等同 **What do you think of ~?**（你覺得～如何？）這種說法，而後者則等同 **How about ~ing?**（～如何？）的說法。

negative effect on ~ = 對～造成負面影響／properly = 恰當地

「反效果」也可說成 adverse effect，e.g. Working out too much can have an adverse effect on your health.（過度運動可能會對身體健康有反效果）。

click-rate = 點閱率／banner ad = 橫幅廣告

「煩人的橫幅廣告」可說成 annoying banner ad，e.g. I don't know how to prevent these annoying banner ads.（我不知道該怎麼防堵這些煩人的橫幅廣告）。

no matter what ~ = 無論～；不管～／underestimate = 低估；小看／impact = 影響力；效果

「電視強大的影響力」也可說成 the powerful grip of TV。另，「高估」說成 overestimate。

word of mouth = 口碑；口耳相傳／definitely = 確定地／work wonders = 達成奇蹟般的效果

「以口耳相傳的方式宣傳～」可說成 promote ~ by word of mouth；「透過口耳相傳散佈出去」說成 spread through word of mouth；「關於～的口傳資訊」則說成 word-of-mouth information on ~。

Skit
企劃開發篇 ————————————————

企劃案通過?不通過?截然不同的兩名企劃人

Man: **I heard❶ you're going to start** a new project.

Woman: **It's been my dream to get the proposal approved since I joined the company.**

M: **I'm stuck in a rut when it comes to getting new ideas. How did you do it?**

W: **I did marketing research and a questionnaire survey to target a market niche.**

M: **Susan's proposal looked more attractive, but you had a better idea.**

W: **Thanks, but now there's a lot to do. I have to draw up specifications and work out a schedule, and I have to keep it within budget.**

M: **I got my proposal turned down again. This is the fourth time in a row.**

W: **That's too bad❷. You should go out more often to get some inspiration.**

男子：我聽說妳要開始執行一個新專案。

女子：從我進這間公司開始，我就一直夢想著這個企劃案能通過。

男：在構思新點子方面我遇上了瓶頸。妳是怎麼辦到的？

女：我做市場調查和問卷調查，以便對準市場利基。

男：蘇珊的企劃看起來更有吸引力，但是妳的構想比較好。

女：謝謝，不過現在我有好多事要做。我必須擬定規格，並訂出進度表，還得維持不超出預算。

男：我的企劃案又被否決了。已經四連敗了。

女：真慘。你應該更常出門去找點靈感。

【單字片語】

❶ I hear ~：我聽說～。
❷ That's too bad.：真慘。

Quick Check

讓我們一起來複習本章所介紹過的句型！請依據以下中文句子的意思，完成對應的英文句子。（答案就在本頁最下方）

❶ 我們考量各個層面以設定價格。 →P128

We set prices, (   ) various (   ) (   ) (   ).

❷ 我們有了突破性的創新。 →P129

We (   ) (   ) (   ) a (   ) innovation.

❸ 我們結合產品上市，舉辦一場活動。 →P133

We (   ) (   ) a campaign (   ) (   ) (   ) the product (   ).

❹ 基本上，隨意想到的點子往往都無法實現。 →P136

Basically, (   ) ideas often end up (   ) up in (   ).

❺ 如果沒能參加明天的比賽，我所有的努力就都將付諸流水。 →P144

All my efforts will (   ) right (   ) (   ) (   ) if I can't make it to the competition tomorrow.

❻ 這個計畫一定能通過的。 →P144

This plan is sure to (   ) the (   ) (   ).

❼ 想到預算這麼少，我的創意也不禁變得貧乏。 →P146

With such a (   ) budget (   ) (   ), I can't help (   ) (   ) (   ) ideas.

❽ 我對品質有百分之百的信心，但是談到設計，我不知該說些什麼。 →P146

I'm (   ) (   ) (   ) of the quality. But I don't know what to say (   ) (   ) (   ) (   ) the design.

❾ 你知道的，最重要的是團隊精神。 →P148

(   ) (   ) (   ) is teamwork, you know.

❿ 口碑肯定能創造奇蹟。 →P150

(   ) (   ) (   ) definitely (   ) (   ).

---

❶taking/aspects/into/account ❷come/up/with/breakthrough ❸kick/off/in/conjunction/with/launch ❹random/going/smoke ❺go/down/the/drain ❻get/green/light ❼small/ in/mind/running/low/on ❽100/percent/sure/when/it/comes/to ❾What/counts/most ❿Word/of/mouth/works/wonders

chapter 6

休息
Taking a Break

喝杯咖啡喘口氣，
午休時間結伴外出打牙祭，
在茶水間閒話家常聊八卦。
本章便要為你介紹，
上班族們短暫小憩時的各種行為，
以及心中的想法。

Words 單字篇

❽眼藥水

❾茶水間
❿八卦；閒話

❶喘息
❷短暫休息
❸員工休息室

❹自動販賣機
❺公司福利社

❼老煙槍

❻吸煙區

⓫午飯時間

⓬員工餐廳

⓯今日午餐
⓰A套餐

⓭餐廳
⓮小吃店

⓱飲食攤

❶breather ❷break ❸staff room ❹vending machine ❺company shop ❻smoking area ❼heavy smoker ❽eyedrops ❾staff kitchen ❿gossip ⓫lunchtime ⓬company cafeteria ⓭restaurant ⓮diner

首先，就讓我們透過各種事、物的名稱，
來掌握「休息」給人的整體印象。

⑳自動提款機

㉑屋頂

㉓化妝　　　㉒廁所；洗手間

⑲水電瓦斯費帳單
⑱跑腿；差使

㉔點心
㉕午睡；打盹

⑮daily lunch special　⑯A meal-set　⑰food stand　⑱errand
⑲utility bill　⑳cash machine　㉑rooftop　㉒restroom　㉓makeup
㉔snack　㉕nap

1 我喝杯茶喘口氣。
I take a breather over a cup of tea.

2 我從自動販賣機（在公司福利社）買飲料。
I get a drink <u>from the vending machine</u> (<u>at the company shop</u>).

3 我在員工休息室抽根菸。
I have a smoke in the staff room.

4 我滴一些眼藥水。
I put in some eyedrops.

5 我和同事一起去員工餐廳吃飯。
I go for lunch at the company cafeteria with my colleague[s].

tips

❶ breather 是「喘息；喘氣」之意，take a breather 就是「休息一下；喘口氣」。而此例句也可說成 I have a tea break.。
❸ 「飯後一根煙」就說成 after-meal cigarette，而「我們去休息一下吧」則可說成 Let's have a break.。
❻ 「為了避免排隊⋯」可說成 ... to avoid a long line。

158 身 體 動 作 篇

6　我錯開午餐時間以免人擠人。
I shift my lunch hour to avoid the crowd.

7　我大老遠地到下一個車站去吃午餐。
I go all the way to the next station to have lunch.

8　我請某個人〔在我不在的時候〕幫忙接電話。
I ask someone else to handle the phone calls [while I'm gone].

9 我叫午餐外送。
I have my lunch delivered.

10 我去散個步轉換心情。
I take a walk for a change.

❼ go all the way to ~ 就是「大老遠特地去～」。
❽ handle 是「處理～；應付～」之意。
❾ have ~ delivered 就是「請人送～來」的意思。
❿ for a change 是「為了轉換心情」之意。

11 我休息並養精蓄銳，以便應付下午的辛苦工作。
I rest, and get my energy back for the tough work [to come] in the afternoon.

12 我小睡一下。
I take a quick nap.

13 我趴在桌上午睡。
I rest my head on the desk and take a nap.

14 我利用午休時間辦完差事。
I get my errands done during my lunch break.

15 我去自動提款機領錢，以備今晚的酒敘使用。
I get some money out from the cash machine for tonight's after-work drink.

⓫ tough work 就是「辛苦的、累人的工作」。
⓬ nap 是「打盹」之意。
⓭ 此例中的 take a nap 可以用 sleep 代替。
⓮ errand 就是「跑腿辦事」。而「辦完事情」也可說成 I finish what I have to do.（我完成我該做的事）。

16 我刷牙並補妝。
I brush my teeth and freshen up my makeup.

17 我小憩一下，吃個點心。
I take a [short] break to have a snack.

18 我分發（吃）午後點心。
I <u>pass out</u> (<u>eat</u>) afternoon snacks.

19 我在茶水間站著和同事聊八卦（閒聊）。
I stand around <u>gossiping</u> (<u>chatting</u>) with co-workers in the staff kitchen.

⓯ ATM 為 automated teller machine（自動提款機）的縮寫，也可說成 cash machine。

⓰ 「補妝」也可改用 reapply my makeup。

⓲ pass out（分發）也可改用 hand out，兩者意思相同。

⓳ stand around ~ing 就是「站著做～」之意。此例句也可簡化為 I <u>gossip</u>/<u>chat</u> with co-workers。

1 做到一個段落就可以休息一下了。

Take a break when things have settled down a bit.

2 你當然可以偶爾休息一下。

You deserve a break from time to time.

3 你應該要常常讓眼睛休息,否則會因為盯著螢幕太久而造成眼睛過度疲勞。

You should rest your eyes frequently, or you will strain your eyes from staring at the computer screen for too long.

4 她突然不見蹤影,跑到洗手間去打瞌睡。

She suddenly disappeared, taking a nap in the restroom.

5 我要去弄杯咖啡來提神。

I'll get a cup of coffee to wake me up.

6 現今要找個可以抽煙的地方都不容易。

Nowadays I have trouble finding places where smoking is not prohibited.

take a break = 休息一下；稍事休息／things have settled down = 事情已告一段落 ／a bit = 稍微；有點

「做到一個段落時」也可説成 when you think it's OK to stop what you are doing（當你覺得可以停下手邊工作時）。

---

deserve = 應得～／break = 休息；小憩／from time to time = 不時；偶爾

此例句也可説成 You need to relax once in a while.（你偶爾也該放鬆一下）。

---

rest = 使休息／frequently = 頻繁地；經常地／strain = 因過度使用而損傷／stare at ~ = 盯著～／computer screen = 電腦螢幕

此例句也可説成 You will get eyestrain if you keep staring at the computer screen.（若你仍一直盯著螢幕看，是會造成眼睛疲勞的）。

---

suddenly = 突然／disappear = 消失／take a nap = 午睡／restroom = 洗手間；化妝室；廁所

此例前半句也可改為 She was suddenly nowhere in sight（她突然不見人影），而後半句中的 restroom 可用 bathroom（浴室；洗手間）代替。

---

get a cup of coffee = 去弄杯咖啡來／wake ~ up = 叫醒～；使～打起精神

「我要煮些咖啡以便保持清醒」可説成 I'll make some coffee to keep myself awake.。

---

nowadays = 現今／have trouble ~ing = 做～的時候遇到困難／not prohibited = 不被禁止的

此例句也可説成 Nowadays it's very difficult to find places where I can smoke.（現在很難找到可以讓我抽煙的地方）。

7　我覺得他在吸煙區晃蕩的時間比在辦公室還長很多，因為他是個老煙槍。

I think he hangs around in the smoking area much longer than in the office because he's such a heavy smoker.

8　今天是發薪日，所以咱們午餐吃點好吃的吧！

It's payday, so let's eat something nice for lunch!

9　我老闆找我一起吃午餐，這非常難得。我猜他一定有什麼事。

My boss asked me out for lunch, which is very rare. I suspect there must be something up with him.

10　我對常去的店已經厭煩了，所以我今天可能會試試不同的店。

I'm rather tired of the usual restaurant, so I may try a different one today.

11　到處都好擠，搞不好我會吃不到午餐呢！

Every place is so crowded that maybe I won't get to eat my lunch!

12　如果在這裡排隊等待，我的午休時間就要結束了！

If I wait in line here, my lunch break will be over!

hang around = 徘徊；流連／smoking area = 吸煙區 cf. non-smoking area = 禁煙區／much longer than ~ = 比~還長很多／heavy smoker = 老煙槍
「戒煙」可説成 <u>quit</u>/<u>stop</u>/<u>give up</u> smoking。

---

payday = 發薪日 cf. pay = 薪水；報酬／eat something nice = 吃點好吃的東西
「午餐吃點特別的」説成 eat something special for lunch，而「豪華午餐」則説成 splendid lunch。

---

ask ~ out for ... = 找~出去… e.g. ask ~ out for a date = 邀請~去約會／rare = 罕見的；稀有的／I suspect = 我猜想~；我懷疑~／there must be something up = 一定有什麼事
此例第一句中的 which 是指 My boss asked me out for lunch = 我老闆找我一起去吃午飯一這整件事。

---

be tired of ~ = 對~感到厭煩 cf. be fed up with ~ = 對~覺得很膩／usual = 平常的；通常的／a different one = 不同的東西（這裡的 one 指 restaurant）
此例句也可説成 I've had enough of the usual restaurant, so I may try a new one today.（我已受夠常去的店了，所以我今天可能會試間新的店）。

---

every place = 每個地方（every ~ 視為單數，故動詞用 is）／crowded = 擁擠的／not get to eat ~ = 吃不到~
此例句的前半部也可説成 All the restaurants are so crowded（所有餐廳都人滿為患）。

---

wait in line = 排隊等待／lunch break = 午休／be over = 結束
此例句中的 wait in line 可改用 stand in line（排隊；站成一排）。lunch break 可改用 luch hour。

13 這個價格還包含甜點？這家店的今日午餐還真是划算。
This price includes dessert? The daily lunch special at this restaurant is really reasonable.

14 我已經等這麼久了，但是我的 A 套餐依舊還沒來。
I've been waiting for so long, but my A meal-set still isn't here yet.

15 我只有 100 元可以吃午餐，所以 50 元的漢堡真的幫了大忙。
I only have 100 NT-dollars for lunch, so 50-NT-dollar burgers are really helpful.

16 我常在那個攤子吃麵。
I often have noodles at that food stand.

17 哎呀！麵湯噴到我的領帶上了。
Oops! I splashed the noodle soup on my tie!

18 我都自己做午餐，這樣才能吃得營養均衡。
I make my own lunch so that I can eat a well-balanced meal.

include = 包含／dessert = 甜點／daily lunch special = 今日午餐（daily = 每日的）／reasonable = 合理的；價錢公道的
本例的 reasonable 即 cheap （便宜）、inexpensive（不貴）之意。

---

for so long = 這麼久／A meal-set = A 套餐／still isn't here yet = 依然還沒來
「我午飯吃的是套餐」可說成 I have a set meal for lunch.。

---

burger = 漢堡／helpful = 有幫助的
本例中的 burger 為 hamburger 之略。另，「薯條」叫 fries。

Have = 吃／noodles = 麵（通常用複數）／food stand = 飲食攤
本例句中的 have 可用 eat 代替。

Oops! = 哎呀！／splash = 潑灑；噴濺／noodle soup = 麵湯／tie = 領帶
「速食麵、泡麵」為 instant noodles。

---

make one's lunch = 自己做午餐／eat a meal = 用餐／well-balanced meal = 營養均衡的飲食
此例也可改為 I want to eat healthy, so I prepare my own lunch.。

19 今天天氣真好！我想到屋頂上去吃午餐。
It's such a nice day! I'd like to have lunch on the rooftop.

20 你真幸運有一位每天幫你裝便當的太太！
You are so lucky to have a wife who packs your lunch every day!

21 其實，我很想一個人吃午飯，但是我必須和別人交際應酬。
Actually, I'd like to have lunch by myself, but I have to socialize with others.

22 邊吃邊聊工作，會消化不良。
It's not good for digestion if you talk about work while eating.

23 午餐時間是交換資訊的絕佳時機。
Lunch hour is a great time to exchange information.

24 也許我現在該上網看看那個有趣的新聞。
Maybe I should check out that interesting news on the Net right now.

It's such a nice day! = 今天天氣真好！／I'd like to ~ = 我想要～／rooftop = 屋頂

「天氣好的日子」除了用 nice day 外，也可用 sunny day（晴朗的日子）、beautiful day（美好的日子）等說法。

---

lucky = 幸運的／so ~ to... = 如此～能有…／pack one's lunch = 裝便當

此例句中 pack your lunch 可用 prepare your lunch（準備你的便當）代替。

---

actually = 其實／by myself = 自己一個人／socialize with ~ = 和～交際應酬

此例也可說成 To tell the truth, I prefer to have my lunch alone, but I need to eat with others to socialize. 。

---

digestion = 消化／talk about work = 談論工作／while eating = 在吃東西的時候

此例也可說成 Talking about business while eating will upset your stomach.（吃東西的時候談工作，會弄壞你的胃）。

---

lunch hour = 午飯時間 cf. lunch break = 午休／a great time to ~ = 做～的絕佳時機／exchange information = 交換資訊

「我在午休時與別人交換了資訊」，可說成 I exchanged information with others during lunch break. 。

---

check out ~ = 查看～／on the Net = 在網路上

本例中的 Net 指的就是 Internet.。「我透過網路取得最新資訊」就說成 I get the newest information from/through the Internet. 。

25 每次來送我們訂的披薩的那個小弟怎麼了？

What happened to the pizza boy who always delievered the pizza we ordered?

26 本週輪到我在午休時間負責接電話。

It's my turn to watch the phone during lunch-hour this week.

27 我想要有效率地運用午休時間準備資格考。

I want to use my lunch break effectively to study for the qualifying test.

28 如果我能在午飯時間小睡個 10 分鐘，那麼下午工作起來就會有效率得多。

If I can take a 10-minute nap during lunchtime, then I'll be able to work much better in the afternoon.

29 洗手間擠滿了刷牙和補妝的女人。

The restroom is crowded with women brushing their teeth and reapplying their makeup.

30 那個女孩在午休時把她的妝全都卸掉。

That girl takes off all her makeup during lunch break.

What happened to ~? = 怎麼了？／pizza boy = 送披薩的小弟／deliver = 配送／order = 訂購

注意，What happened? 指「發生了什麼事？」，而 What happened to ~ 則是「～怎麼了？」之意。

It's my turn to ~ = 輪到我做～（turn = 順序）／watch the phone = 看顧電話

本例中的 watch the phone 也可用 answer the phone calls（接聽電話）或 handle the phone call（處理電話應對）等說法來表達。

---

use ~ to ... = 利用～來做…／effectively = 有效率地／study for ~ = 為了～而唸書／qualifying test = 資格考

此例句也可說成 I want to get the most out of my lunch break by studying for the qualifying test.。

---

take a nap = 午睡／10-minute = 10 分鐘的／much better = 好得多

「你該停下來休息」可說成 You should stop and rest.。

---

restroom = 化妝室；洗手間 cf. 洗手台 = wash stand／be crowded with ~ = 被～擠滿／brush one's teeth = 刷牙／reapply one's makeup = 補妝（makeup = 化妝）

此例前半的「洗手間擠滿了女人」也可說成 The restroom is <u>full of</u>/<u>filled with</u> women。

---

take off one's makeup = 卸妝 cf. 也可說成 remove one's makeup

「化妝」說成 put on makeup，「化妝品」則是 cosmetics。而「我得補個妝才行」就說成 I need to fix up my makeup.。

31 我應該趁午休時間去付一下水電瓦斯費帳單。
I should pay the utility bills during the lunch hour.

32 午餐時間郵局總是大排長龍。
The line at the post office is so long at lunchtime.

33 這兒有一些天鶴公司送來的糖果餅乾！可以麻煩你分送給會計部的每個人嗎？
Here are some sweets from Crane company! Could you pass them around to everyone in the accounting department?

34 我同事帶來了一些冰淇淋分送給大家。
My colleague brought some ice cream to pass around.

35 當我覺得心情低落時，巧克力總是能讓我振作起來。
When I feel down, chocolate can always cheer me up.

36 這陣子，我工作的時候吃了太多零食。
These days I'm snacking too much during work.

utility bill ＝ 水電瓦斯費帳單 （utility ＝〔水、電、瓦斯等〕公用事業）
「轉帳付款」說成 pay through a bank transfer，而「網路轉帳」則說成
online transfer over the Internet。

---

line ＝ 排隊隊伍／post office ＝ 郵局／so long ＝ 如此的長／lunchtime ＝ 午餐
時間
「我在郵局排著長隊」可說成 I stand in a long line at the post office.。

---

here are ～ ＝ 這裡有～／sweets ＝ 糖果；甜食（多用複數）／pass ～ around
＝ 分送～／accounting department ＝ 會計部
在美國「糖果」多用 candy 表示。

---

colleague ＝ 同事／brought ＝ 帶來了（bring 的過去式和過去分詞）／ice
cream ＝ 冰淇淋
「帶～給某人」用 bring sb.～ 表示，e.g.「我帶了一些三明治給你」說成 I
brought you some sandwiches.。

---

feel down ＝ 覺得心情低落／cheer one up ＝ 讓人振作起來
本例前半句也可說成 When I am down.。

---

these days ＝ 這陣子 cf. lately 或 recently ＝ 最近／snack ＝ 吃零食（snack
做為名詞就是「零嘴；點心」之意）／during work ＝ 在工作的時候。
「在正餐之間吃零食」可說成 snack/eat between meals。

37 如果你跟她說了些什麼，那麼隔天一定會傳遍整個辦公室。

If you tell her something, then the next day it'll be all over the office.

38 這些女孩聊八卦聊得這麼大聲。我是否該告訴她們，我們全都聽得一清二楚呢？

These girls are gossiping so loudly. Should I tell them that we can hear everything they are talking about?

the next day = 隔天；第二天／all over the office = 遍及整個辦公室

此例的後半句也可説成 then the next day everyone in the office will know about it.（那麼隔天辦公室裡的每個人都會知道這件事）。

---

gossip = 聊八卦；説閒話（gossip 做為名詞就是「八卦傳聞；閒言閒語」之意）／loudly = 大聲地／Should I ~? = 我是否該～？

「他守不住秘密」可説成 He can't keep his mouth shut. ，而「大嘴巴；口無遮攔的人」就叫 big mouth。

Skit  休息篇

美食最能振奮人心！發薪日的午餐，吃什麼好呢？

Woman: **It's payday, so let's have something special for lunch.**

Man: **I'm going to have my lunch delivered. It's my turn to watch the phone during lunch this week.**

W: **Actually❶, I should pay my utility bills, but the line at the post office is so long at lunchtime. If I stand in line there, my lunch hour will be over.**

M: **Why don't you❷ have some sandwiches? That's quick❸.**

W: **But it's dreary❹ to eat sandwiches at the office.**

M: **Every shop is so crowded you might not even get to eat lunch.**

W: **I could shift my lunch hour to avoid the crowds but I don't like to eat alone.**

M: **If you wait till one o'clock, I can go with you.**

W: **Really? That would be great!❺**

女子：今天是發薪日，所以咱們午餐吃點好吃的吧！

男子：我要叫午餐外送。本週輪到我在午休時間負責接電話。

女：其實，我應該去付一下水電瓦斯費帳單，但是午餐時間郵局總是大排長龍。如果我在那裡排隊等待，我的午休時間就要結束了！

男：妳何不吃三明治？那很快喔。

女：但是在辦公室吃三明治感覺好淒涼。

男：每間店都好擠，妳搞不好會吃不到午餐呢！

女：我可以錯開午餐時間以免人擠人，但是我不喜歡一個人吃飯。

男：如果妳等到一點，我就可以跟你一起去。

女：真的嗎？那真是太好了！

【單字片語】

❶ actually：事實上；其實

❷ Why don't you ~?：你何不～？

❸ quick：快的；迅速的

❹ dreary：淒涼的；憂鬱的

❺ That would be great!：那真是太好了！

Quick Check

讓我們一起來複習本章所介紹過的句型！請依據以下中文句子的意思，完成對應的英文句子。（答案就在本頁最下方）

❶ 我去散個步轉換心情。 →P159

I ( ) a walk ( ) ( ) ( ).

❷ 我利用午休時間辦完差事。 →P160

I ( ) my ( ) ( ) during my lunch break.

❸ 我刷牙並補妝。 →P161

I ( ) my teeth and ( ) ( ) my ( ).

❹ 我分發午後點心。 →P161

I ( ) ( ) ( ) ( ).

❺ 你當然可以偶爾休息一下。 →P162

You ( ) a break ( ) ( ) ( ) ( ).

❻ 她突然不見蹤影，跑到洗手間去打瞌睡。 →P162

She suddenly ( ), ( ) a ( ) in the restroom.

❼ 現今連要找個可以抽煙的地方都不容易。 →P162

Nowadays I ( ) ( ) finding places where smoking is not
( ).

❽ 我對常去的店已經厭煩了，故我今天可能會試試不同的店。 →P164

I'm rather ( ) ( ) the usual restaurant, so I may
( ) a different one today.

❾ 每次來送我們訂的披薩的那個小弟怎麼了？ →P170

( ) ( ) ( ) the pizza boy who always delivered
the pizza we ordered?

❿ 如果妳跟她說了些什麼，那麼隔天一定會傳遍整個辦公室。 →P174

If you tell her something, then the next day it'll ( ) ( )
( ) the office.

---

❶take/for/a/change ❷get/errands/done time ❻disappeared/taking/nap ❼have/
❸brush/freshen/up/makeup ❹pass/out/ trouble/prohibited ❽tired/of/try ❾what/
afternoon/snacks ❺deserve/from/time/to/ happened/to ❿ be/all/over

會議
Meetings

 會議中，
免不了各式各樣的爭論、唇槍舌戰，
但在此我們著重的並非表面發言，
而是聚焦於會議中浮現於人內心的
「真正想法」。

Words 單字篇

❶（一般）會議
❷聚會；聯歡會
❸（大型的）會議
❹大會；集會

❺討論
❻談判；協商

❼主席

❽討論主持人

⓬出席者；
與會者

⓭水瓶

⓫會議記錄
❾議程
❿主題

❶meeting ❷get-together ❸conference ❹convention ❺discussion
❻negotiation ❼chairperson ❽facilitator ❾agenda ❿subject
⓫minutes ⓬attendee ⓭jug ⓮meeting room ⓯whiteboard

首先，就讓我們透過各種事、物的名稱，
來掌握「會議」給人的整體印象。

⑳雷射筆
⑲指示棒
⑮白板
㉑簡報者
⑯麥克筆
⑱螢幕
⑰投影機
㉒會議資料
㉓簡報資料
㉔參考資料
㉕有建設性的建議
⑭會議室

⑯marker　⑰projector　⑱screen　⑲pointer rod　⑳laser pointer
㉑presenter　㉒handout　㉓presentation material　㉔reference
material　㉕constructive suggestion

 **chapter 7** Meetings

1　我安排會議。
I arrange a meeting.

2　我點數出席人數。
I count the number of attendees.

3　我通知相關人員會議的時間安排。
I notify the people concerned of the meeting schedule.

4　我送出提醒用的電子郵件。
I send an e-mail reminder.

5　我找出上一次會議尚未解決的事項。
I find out what was left open during the last meeting.

tips

❷「點名」可說成 do a roll call 或 take attendance。
❸ 寫在電子郵件開頭處的「敬啟者」就說成 To whom it may concern。
❹ remind ~ of ... 可用來表達「提醒～關於…」之意，e.g. The e-mail reminded me of the meeting.（這封電子郵件提醒了我關於開會的事）。

6　我事先發送議程給相關人員。
I send an agenda in advance to the people concerned.

7　我安排座位。
I create a seating arrangement.

8　我事先準備好所有設備。
I have all the equipment ready beforehand.

9　我準備了足夠份數的會議資料。
I prepare the required number of handouts for the meeting.

10　我花了一番心思準備資料。
I put a lot of thought into the arrangement of the materials.

❺ 「尚未解決的事項；待決議事項」也可說成 pending matter。
❻ in advance 就是「事先」，和 ❽ 的 beforehand（預先）意思相同。
❾ hand out ~ 是「將～用手遞出」之意。而「在會議上〔傳遞〕分發資料」可說成 I pass out handouts in the meeting.。
❿ put a lot of thought into ~ 就是「對～花了好一番心思」。

11 我事先閱讀資料。
I read up on the material beforehand.

12 我為這場大型會議做準備工作。
I lay the groundwork for the conference.

13 我安排電話視訊會議。
I arrange a video teleconference.

14 我主持會議。
I chair a meeting.

15 我引導討論。
I facilitate a discussion.

tips

⓫ read up on ~ 就是「研讀～；預習～」之意。

⓬ lay the groundwork for~ 指「為～做準備」。

⓭ 「和～進行電話會議」可說成 teleconference with ~。

⓯ 在會議中引導討論的人就說成 facilitator。facilitate 的原意為「使～容易；促進」，e.g. This software facilicates my work.

16 我鼓勵某人發言。
I prompt someone to speak out.

17 我請求某人提供意見。
I call on someone to offer a comment.

18 我中斷了某人的發言。
I cut someone off.

19 我將討論拉回原來的主題。
I bring the discussion back on track.

20 我努力協調不同的看法。
I try to coordinate different views.

（這個軟體讓我的工作變得更容易）。

⑰ give ~ the floor 可表達「給予～發言的空間（機會）」之意。

⑱ 「忽視～〔的發言〕」可用 pass ~ over，e.g. The facilitator passed her over and kept talking.（主持人忽視她的發言並繼續講話）。

⑲ track 原指「軌道、路線」，在此則指「討論的主軸」。Am I on the right track? 就是「我沒岔題吧？」之意。

21 我說明這個計畫的概要。
I give an outline explanation of the plan.

22 我們都各自提出構想。
We all pitch in ideas.

23 我們照順時針方向依序進行簡報。
We make presentations going around clockwise.

24 我們進入質詢與回答時間。
We begin a question-and-answer session.

25 我們交換意見。
We exchange opinions.

tips

㉑ 此例句也可說成 I give a brief overview of the plan.。
㉒ 「合力出錢」說成 chip in，e.g. Why don't we all chip in and buy a coffee maker?（我們何不一起出錢買一台咖啡機？）。
㉓ 「逆時針方向」說成 counterclockwise。
㉔ 在質詢與回答時間「接受～的發問」就說成 take questions

26 我指出問題點。
I point out a problem.

27 我提出相反的意見。
I give an opposing opinion.

28 我們達成協議。
We reach an agreement.

29 我們尋求折衷方案。
We seek a compromise.

30 我做會議記錄。
I take the minutes.

from ~，e.g. Now I'm going to take a few questions from the audience.（現在我將接受聽眾的發問）。

㉗「贊同的意見」說成 favorable opinion。

㉙ Let's meet each other halfway here. 便是「在此讓我們各退一步」的意思。

31 我做筆記。
I take notes.

32 我努力不打哈欠。
I try hard not to yawn.

33 我在會議中偷偷做些別的事。
I work on some other stuff during a meeting.

tips

㉛ 「公司內部傳閱用的備忘錄」叫 memo（= memorandum）。

㉜ 「我假裝我有在聽」說成 I act like I'm listening.。

㉞ 「休息 10 分鐘〔喝杯咖啡／上個廁所〕」可用 have a 10-minute [coffee/bathroom] break。

㉟ Let's continue where we left off. 就是「讓我們從剛剛中斷的

34 我們暫停休息。
We pause for a break.

35 我們重新開始會議。
We resume the meeting.

36 我們進行投票表決。
We take a vote.

地方繼續」。

③ vote <u>for</u> (<u>against</u>) ~ 就是「針對～進行投票表決（贊成／反對）」。

189

1 為什麼大家總是要花這麼久時間才能到齊開會？
How come everyone always takes so long to get together for the meeting?

---

2 首先，我們每個人都必須同意本次會議的共同目標。
First of all, we each have to share the common objective of the meeting.

---

3 每個人都拿到資料了嗎？
Everyone's got a handout now?

---

4 我覺得這簡報資料恐怕無法讓人留下深刻印象。
I'm afraid the presentation material won't make much of an impression.

---

5 他真是沒用！來開會竟然什麼參考資料都沒準備。
He's so useless! He shows up for a meeting without any reference materials or data.

---

6 我想，PowerPoint 或資料的可看性也會影響你簡報的結果成敗。
The result of your presentation depends also on the viewability of your PowerPoint or material, I think.

How come S + V? = 為什麼～？／get together = 集合；聚集

get-together 有「聚會；聯歡會」的意思，e.g. We're having a get-together to welcome Mr. Newman on Friday.（我們週五將舉辦一個歡迎會來歡迎紐曼先生）。

---

first of all = 首先／share = 共有；同意〔觀點、感受〕／common objective = 共同目標

「共通的理解」可說成 common understanding，e.g. The director affirmed the common understanding of the project.（主管確認了〔大家〕對此專案的共通理解）。

---

handout = 會議資料

handout 就是「〔會議、演講等場合所分發的〕參考資料」。「你還有多的參考資料嗎？」可說成 Do you have some extra handouts?。

I'm afraid ～ =〔我覺得〕恐怕～／presentation material = 簡報資料

not make much of ～ 就是「不會造成很大的～」之意，e.g. It won't make much of a difference to our workload.（這不會讓我們的工作量產生太大差異）。

---

useless = 沒用的；無能的／show up for ～ = 現身～；出席～／reference material = 參考資料

「沒用；一無是處」也可用 be good for nothing 來表達，e.g. Forgot everything discussed in the meeting? You're good for nothing!（會議所討論的你全都忘了？你真是一無是處！）。

---

depend on ～ = 取決於～；依靠～／viewability = 可看性；可視性

形容詞 viewable 為「可看見的；易看的」之意，同義詞為 easy-to-read（易讀的）。另，eye-friendly 指「對眼睛好的；不傷眼的」，e.g. The monitor is eye-friendly.（這個螢幕不傷眼）。

7 在會議裡宣讀那些數字毫無意義。那是浪費時間。

Reading out all those figures in a meeting is pointless. It's a waste of time.

8 好簡報的關鍵就在於要有吸引人的東西。

The main thing in a good presentation is having a good hook.

9 由於他說話大聲且口齒清晰，所以他的話很容易聽懂。

He's easy to listen to because he speaks with a loud voice and clear enunciation.

10 他的發言總是簡明扼要。

His speeches are always clear-cut and to the point.

11 我懂了。現在我有了不同的看法。

I see. Now I'm looking at it in a different way.

12 就他一個人講了好一陣子。

He's been the only guy speaking up for a while.

read out ~ = 宣讀／figure = 數字／pointless = 毫無意義的／waste of time = 浪費時間

pointless 的 point 是指「重點；意義」，e.g. The point is you should give your opinion.（重點在於你應該要提出你的意見）。

---

the main thing = 主要的事／hook = 吸引人的東西；誘人的特點

hook 原為「掛鉤」之意。而 hook 的常見用法還有 let ~ off the hook（擺脫～的責任），e.g. My supervisor let me off the hook with a mild reprimand.（我的上司用溫和的譴責讓我脫身）。

---

with a loud voice = 大聲地／enunciation = 口齒清晰

「很清晰的聲音」可說成 carrying voice，其中的 carry 就是「〔聲、音〕傳遞；傳達」的意思，e.g. The presenter spoke in a carrying voice so I felt comfortable listening to her.（由於這位簡報者用很清晰的聲音說話，所以聽她說話我感覺很舒適）。

---

clear-cut = 清楚的；明確的／to the point = 扼要的

相反的「離題的；不切題的」則說成 off the point，e.g. His argument tends to be off the point.（他的論點很容易離題）。

I see = 我懂了。／in a different way = 以別的方式；以不同的感覺

「恍然大悟；茅塞頓開」可說成 The scales fell from my eyes.，其中的 scale 原本指「鱗片」。而「跳脫框架思考」可說成 think outside the box，e.g. Let's think outside the box and come up with a better plan.（讓我們跳脫框架思考，想出一個更好的計劃）。

---

speak up = 發表意見；發言／for a while = 一段時間；一陣子

「講個不停」可說成 talk nonstop，e.g. She talked nonstop for 30 minutes.（她連續講了 30 分鐘都沒停過）。另外，諺語 The greatest talkers are the least doers. 指「話多的人，事做得少」。

13 我真的聽不懂你在說什麼。
I really don't get what you're saying here.

14 你發言之前何不先動動腦？
Why don't you engage your brain before speaking?

15 我很好奇這討論最後的結局為何。
I wonder where this discussion is going to end up.

16 你聽到他剛剛說的話嗎？很顯然他根本搞不清楚狀況。
Hear what he just said? Obviously, he can't even see what's going on.

17 哇，這發言真的沒辦法寫進會議記錄裡。
Wow, I can't put this word down in the minutes.

18 由於我的簡報明顯地結束得很草率，他們把我電得很慘。
Because my presentation obviously slacked off towards the end, they really grilled me.

get (= understand) = 理解

「了解～的主旨」可用 follow the gist of ～ 來表達，e.g. Apparently, the chief was not following the gist of your speech.（很顯然長官並沒有聽懂你話中的要點）。

Why don't you ~? = 何不～？／engage one's brain = 動腦思考

「釐清思緒」説成 organize one's thoughts，e.g. You should organize your thoughts before writing e-mail.（撰寫電子郵件之前，你應該要先釐清自己的思緒）。

---

end up ~ = 結果變成～；以～告終

end up ~ 用來表達「以～的狀態結束」之意，e.g. The event ended up failing.（這活動最終以失敗收場）。另外，「最後不了了之」則可説成 end up in the air。

---

obviously = 很明顯地／what's going on? = 發生了什麼事

「掃興的人；白目的人」可用 wet blanket（濕掉的毛毯）來形容，e.g. He's such a wet blanket, offering only negative feedback.（他真是個白目王，只會提供負面意見）。

---

put ~ down = 寫進～／minutes = 會議記錄

「把～寫下；把～記下」也可用 write ~ down 或 take ~ down 等説法。「〔在會議中〕做會議記錄」則説成 take minutes，e.g. I think I need to work on how to take minutes.（我想我得多學學怎麼寫會議記錄）。

---

slack off towards the end = 結束得很草率；虎頭蛇尾／grill = 炮火猛烈地質問

slack off 也經常用來表示「懈怠」之意，e.g. Don't slack off.（別鬆懈）。而 grill（放在烤架上用火燒烤）這個動詞，在會話中常用來表達「連續不停地質問」之意。

19 只要是由赫許先生主持討論，會議總是能順利進行。
Meetings always go smoothly when Mr. Hush is the facilitator.

20 有史坦先生參與會議，大家就都會正襟危坐。
With Mr. Stern in a meeting, everyone sits bolt upright.

21 經理講話經常會離題。
The manager gets off the subject so often.

22 你能不能想出點更有建設性的建議？
Couldn't you come up with some more constructive suggestions?

23 這根本就是舊計劃的改版而已嘛。
This is a total rehash of the previous plan.

24 自上次的會議之後，此事毫無進展。
Nothing on this matter has made progress since the last meeting.

facilitator = 討論主持人

「主持會議」說成 chair a meeting。

---

with ~ = 有～在／sit bolt upright = 坐得直挺挺的；正襟危坐

「打破僵局；打破冷場」可說成 break the ice，e.g. Ms. Jordan broke the ice with a joke.（喬丹小姐用一個笑話打破了僵局）。

---

get off the subject = 離題（subject 指「主題」）

「偏離主題」也可說成 stray off the subject。另外，sidetrack 指「使轉移目標、注意力」，e.g. Don't get sidetracked by minute details.（不要讓小細節轉移了注意力）。注意，此句中的 minute 指「微小的」，發音為 [maɪˋnjut]。

Couldn't you ~? = 你能不能～？／come up with ~ = 想出～／constructive = 有建設性的

此例句中的 constructive 也可置換為 practical（實用的）、helpful（有用的）、productive（有生產力的）。

---

rehash = 老調重彈／previous = 以前的

「沿用的、重複使用的構想」也可用 recycled（回收再利用的）來形容，e.g. That's nothing but a recycled idea with a couple of twists.（那不過是稍微加工過的老調重彈罷了）。

---

make progress = 取得進展／since ~ = 從～起就一直

progress 經常用來表達「進展情況；進度」之意，e.g. I have to report the progress of the project to my boss.（我必須向我老闆報告專案進度）。

25 經理從來都不聽手下員工的意見。
The manager never listens to his staff's opinions.

26 聲音大的似乎總能吵得贏。
The squeaky wheel always seems to win in discussions.

27 那有點不切實際，不是嗎？
That's a bit pie in the sky, isn't it?

28 如果沒有數字化的證據，你的說明就不會有說服力。
Your explanation won't be persuasive without numerical evidence.

29 大家都興奮得不得了，開始一個接著一個地講，徹底趕走了我的瞌睡蟲。
Everyone got excited as hell and just started speaking one after another, which really shook off my sleepiness.

30 事情的兩面我都充分理解了，不過還是…。
I appreciate both sides of the situation, but still ....

manager = 經理／listen to ～ = 傾聽〔意見〕

「一般員工」説成 rank-and-filer，e.g. The management usually doesn't think highly of the views of the rank-and-filers.（管理階層通常都不重視一般員工的看法）。

---

squeaky wheel = 聲音大的人；會吵的人／win = 贏

squeaky wheel 字面上的意思是「吱吱作響的車輪」。有句常用諺語就説成 The squeaky wheel gets the grease.（吱吱作響的車輪能獲得潤滑油，意即會吵的孩子有糖吃）。

---

pie in the sky = 在空中的派（看得到吃不到）；不切實際的夢想

用到 pie 這個字的諺語還有 It's easy as pie.（易如反掌）、Don't put your finger into another's pie.（勿管他人之事）。

---

explanation = 說明；解釋／persuasive = 有說服力的／numerical evidence = 數字化的證據

「有説服力的説明」可説成 convincing explanation，而相反的「沒有説服力的説明」則用 lame explanation。

---

as hell = 非常；極度（相當口語的講法）／one after another = 一個接著一個地／shook off ～ = 擺脫～（shook 是 shake 的過去式）。

在口語中，as hell 常被用來強調令人不愉快之事，e.g. I'm as hungry as hell.（我肚子餓得要命）。

---

appreciate ～ = 充分理解～

「聽取雙方意見」説成 hear both sides，而「對～有發言權」則可用 have a say in ～ 來表達，e.g. I have a say in this matter.（對於這件事，我有發言權）。

31 請切入正題。
Cut to the chase, please.

32 讓我把話說完，好嗎？
Let me finish, will you?

33 不知為何，情勢似乎對我們不利。
I don't know why, but the odds seem against us now.

34 很好！討論依照計畫進行。
Good! The discussion proceeded as planned.

35 討論陷入原地打轉。我們應該先暫停，稍後再重新開始。
The discussion is going in circles. We should stop now and make a fresh start later.

36 我們何不就此結束？
Why don't we wrap it up now?

cut to the chase = 直接切入主題

類似的表達方式還有 get down to brass tacks（言歸正傳）。而相反的「拐彎抹角」可說成 beat around the bush，e.g. Stop beating around the bush and tell me how you really feel.（別拐彎抹角了，告訴我你真正的感覺吧）。

---

will you? = ～，好嗎？（接在祈使句之後）

「打斷別人的話」可用 cut ~ off 來表達，e.g. I cut her off and changed the topic.（我打斷她的話並改變話題）。

---

odds = 可能性；機會／against = 逆；反對

odds are against ~ 就是「對～不利」之意。另外還有 against all odds（不顧一切；克服萬難）這種說法。另外，「形勢；潮流」可用 tide 這個字，e.g. The tide seems to be turning.（形勢似乎正在轉變）。

---

proceed = 進行／as ~ = 如同～

「結果和計畫的一樣」可說成 turn out as planned。而「縝密的計畫」可用 best-laid plan，e.g. The best-laid plans go astray.（再完美的計畫也可能出錯，意即人算不如天算）。

---

go in circles = 原地打轉／make a fresh start = 重新開始

「回到原點」說成 go back to square one，「從零開始」說成 start from scratch，e.g. I think we should go back to square one and start from scratch.（我認為我們應該回到原點並從零開始）。

Why don't we ~ ? = 我們何不～？／wrap ~ up = 把～結束掉

而「今天就到此為止吧；今天就此收工吧」可說成 Let's call it a day.。

37 投票表決肯定是對我們有利的。

Taking a vote will definitely give us an edge.

---

38 決議又再度被擱置了。

The decision has been put on the back burner again.

---

39 結果，是老闆的一句話結束了整個討論。

As it turned out, what put an end to the discussion was a word from the boss.

---

40 爭論升溫，於是會議便不斷延長。

The debate heated up, so the meeting dragged on and on.

take a vote = 投票表決／definitely = 肯定；絕對／give ~ an edge = 對~有利

「舉手表決」可説成 vote by a show of hands，e.g. We had a vote by a show of hands at the end of the meeting.（我們在會議最後進行了舉手表決）。

---

put ~ on the back burner = 將~延後處理；將~暫時擱置

put ~ on the back burner 字面上的意思是「將~放在後面的火爐上」。而將應解決的問題或該做的決定「置之不理」則可用 put ~ on the shelf 來表達，e.g. The remodeling project has been put on the shelf.（改裝計畫已被束之高閣）。

---

as it turned out ~ = 結果是~／put an end to ~ = 了結~；結束~／a word from the boss = 老闆的一句話

「這件事以和解告終」説成 The matter was settled with a compromise.。

---

heat up = 白熱化；升溫／drag on and on = 不斷延長

「不斷延長」也可用 take forever（沒完沒了）來表達，e.g. The monthly meeting seemed to take forever.（這每月例會似乎開得沒完沒了）。

商務環境中的有效簡報手法

一. 簡報流程與表達句型

簡報（presentation）有大致的流程可遵循，而且在某個程度上，也有不少固定的表達方式可以使用。以下便以 1～5 的順序說明簡報流程，同時列出常用的英語例句。

1. 打招呼，並介紹簡報者

<u>Good morning, everyone./Good afternoon, ladies and gentlemen.</u> My name is .....（各位早安／大家午安。我叫…）

2. 說明簡報的主要目的和整體大綱

Today, I'd like to talk about ... /The purpose of my talk today is ...（今天我要談的是…／我今天發言的目的是…）

I have divided my talk into three parts./I'm going to talk about three areas.（我把我要說的分成了三部分／我將談到三大部分）

3. 針對各要點提出具體的說明、資料和根據等

First, ...（首先，…）

Next, .../Second, ...（接著，…／其次，…）

Finally, ...（最後，…）

4. 總結

I'd like to summarize my main points again.（我想再次總結我所說的幾個要點）

Thank you for <u>your attention/listening</u>.（感謝您的參與／傾聽）

5. 回答疑問

If there are any questions, I'll be glad to answer them.（如果有任何問題，我都很樂意回答）

荒井貴和　Text by Kiwa Arai

二. 簡報的結構與說話方式

　　就整體結構來說，基本上要先清楚解釋簡報的目的，然後再進入具體的要點說明。重點在於：「要從結論開始陳述」。先把重點說出來，再做詳細說明，並提出證據。在將各個要點都解說過一遍後，於簡報最後，可用總結的形式再次提示每個要點。務必在簡報結束前，讓聽眾都能對簡報要點留下深刻印象。此外，簡報基本上都必須用正式的表達方式，要避免以口語化說法，或以過於輕鬆的語氣講話。

　　「說話清楚明確」可說是做簡報時的最基本原則。對自己的英語能力或發言內容缺乏信心時，很容易就會講得太小聲或太快，這只會讓聽的人一頭霧水。要以冷靜的語調加上稍微慢一點的速度發言，大家才容易聽懂。另外身體語言（身體的動作、姿勢、臉部表情等）也很重要。不可總是盯著自己的筆記（講稿）或投影片看，一定要一邊看著聽眾（進行眼神交流）一邊說。

　　「我的英文很差，各位可能會聽不太懂」之類的藉口不僅多餘，也容易讓別人對你的簡報產生先入為主的不良印象，就算只是想表示謙虛，也不該說出這樣的話。

　　為了讓簡報能發揮功效，就要靈活運用視覺化的資料，如 PowerPoint 投影片等工具，讓簡報要點能更清楚地傳達給聽眾。以 PowerPoint 來說，要注意別在一張投影片中塞進太多資訊，否則聽眾會以閱讀投影片的文字或資訊為主，而不在於聽取簡報，如此就本末倒置了。記得，投影片和資料等都只是輔助工具，只要將必要資訊簡潔、有效地呈現出來就好。

　　最後別忘了，一定要在規定的時間內結束簡報。請做好時間分配，並預留足夠的問答時間。在充分準備、事先演練過後，再正式上場吧！

Skit  會議篇 ────────────────

傑克是最理想的會議主持人

Woman: Good! The discussion proceeded as planned. Today's meeting went really well❶.

Man: Meetings always go smoothly when Jack is the facilitator.

W: Yes, he lays the groundwork and his speeches are always clear-cut and to the point.

M: The manager gets off the subject so often, but Jack brings the discussion back on track.

W: I like how we all pitch in ideas and exchange opinions so we can coordinate different views.

M: But it's also important to know when to pause for a break and then resume the meeting.

W: Yes, Jack really knows how to chair a meeting.

M: I think we should take him out for a drink❷. What do you say?❸

女子：很好！討論都照著計畫進行。今天的會議真的進行得很順利。

男子：只要是由傑克主持討論，會議總是能順利進行。

女：沒錯，他會做好準備，發言又總是簡明扼要。

男：經理講話經常會離題，但是傑克會把方向拉回來。

女：我喜歡大家各自提出構想並交換意見的方式，這樣我們就能協調不同
的看法。

男：不過，知道何時該暫停休息，然後再重新開會也是很重要的。

女：對啊，傑克真的很懂得如何主持會議。

男：我想我們應該帶他去喝一杯。你覺得如何？

【單字片語】

❶ go well：進展順利

❷ take ~ out for a drink：帶～去喝一杯

❸ What do you say?：你覺得如何？（用
於邀請，或詢問對方意見的時候）

Quick Check

讓我們一起來複習本章所介紹過的句型！請依據以下中文句子的意思，完成對應的英文句子。（答案就在本頁最下方）

❶ 我找出上一次會議尚未解決的事項。 →P182

I find out what was (　　　　) (　　　　) during the last meeting.

❷ 我花了一番心思準備資料。 →P183

I (　　　) (　　　) (　　　) (　　　) (　　　) into the arrangement of the materials.

❸ 好簡報的關鍵就在於要有吸引人的東西。 →P192

The main thing in a good presentation is having a (　　　) (　　　).

❹ 聲音大的似乎總能吵得贏。 →P198

The (　　　) (　　　) always seems to (　　　) in discussions.

❺ 那有點不切實際，不是嗎？ →P198

That's a bit (　　　) (　　　) (　　　) (　　　), isn't it?

❻ 請切入正題。 →P200

(　　　) (　　　) (　　　) (　　　), please.

❼ 不知為何，情勢似乎對我們不利。 →P200

I don't know (　　　), but the (　　　) seem (　　　) (　　　) now.

❽ 我們何不就此結束？ →P200

(　　　) don't we (　　　) it (　　　) now?

❾ 投票表決肯定是對我們有利的。 →P202

(　　　) (　　　) (　　　) will definitely (　　　) us (　　　) (　　　).

❿ 決議又再度被擱置了。 →P202

The decision has been (　　　) (　　　) (　　　) (　　　) (　　　) again.

---

❶left/open ❷put/a/lot/of/thought ❸good/hook ❹squeaky/wheel/win ❺pie/in/the/sky ❻Cut/to/the/chase ❼why/odds/against/us ❽Why/wrap/up ❾Taking/a/vote/give/an/edge ❿put/on/the/back/burner

chapter 8

公司活動
Company Events

每家公司多少都有些例行活動，
如一般常見的「聚餐」、「尾牙」、
「員工旅遊」等等。
此外，難以避免的「同事婚禮」、「迎
新送舊」等，
也都有許多在參加時用得上的相關表達
句型。

Words 單字篇

❶朝會；晨會　❷講台

❻歡送會　❾聖誕派對
❼迎新會　❿敬酒
❽尾牙

❸新年演說
❹週年慶祝儀式
❺公司歌曲

❶宴會表演

❶morning staff meeting　❷podium　❸New Year's speech
❹anniversary ceremony　❺company song　❻farewell party
❼welcome party　❽end-of-the-year party　❾christmas party
❿toast　❶party trick　⓬inter-division bowling tournament

首先，讓我們透過各種事、物的名稱，
來掌握「公司活動」給人的整體印象。

⑬保齡球場

⑮高爾夫球賽
⑯公司運動會日
⑰員工旅遊
⑱在職訓練
⑲健康檢查
⑳歲末大掃除

㉑賀電
㉒祝賀詞
㉓禮金

⑫部門對抗
保齡球賽

⑭團隊合作

⑬bowling alley ⑭teamwork ⑮golf competition ⑯company sports
day ⑰company trip ⑱on-the-job-training ⑲physical checkup
⑳year-end cleaning ㉑congratulatory telegram ㉒congratulatory
speech ㉓gift money

1 我參加晨會。
I attend a morning staff meeting.

2 我發表新年演說。
I give the New Year's speech.

3 我提議舉杯敬酒。
I propose a toast.

4 我負責舉辦歡送會。
I take charge of the farewell party.

5 我為迎新會預約了餐廳。
I reserve a restaurant for the welcome party.

tips

❸ propose 為「提議」之意。另，toast 是「敬酒；祝酒」之意，也可做為動詞使用，就是「舉杯為～祝賀；為～乾一杯」的意思。

❹ farewell 就是「告別〔的〕」，而 take charge of ~ 是「負責做～」，在此例中也可改用 organize（安排；計畫）來表達。

❺ reserve 是「預約～；預訂～」之意，也可用 make a reservation [at ~]。

6 我在網路上尋找舉辦歡送會用的餐廳。
I look for a restaurant for the farewell party on the Internet.

7 我替經理倒啤酒。
I pour the manager a beer.

8 我擔任尾牙主持人。
I M.C. the end-of-the-year party.

9 我參加聖誕派對。
I go to the Christmas party.

10 我參加公司的高爾夫球賽。
I enter the company golf competition.

❼ 此例句也可說成 I pour a beer for the manager.。
❽ M.C. 是 master of ceremonies（主持人；司儀）的縮寫，後來衍伸
為動詞，可表達「擔任主持人」之意。另外「尾牙」也可說成 year-
end party。
❿ enter 是「進入；參加」之意。

11 我接受在職訓練。
I receive on-the-job training.

12 我做公司為我安排的健康檢查。
I have a physical checkup arranged by the company.

13 我參加同事的婚宴。
I attend my colleague's wedding reception.

14 我集資出錢，幫同事買結婚禮物。
I chip in some money for my co-worker's wedding gift.

tips

⓫ on-the-job 就是「在職」之意。
⓬ 「健康檢查」也可說成 medical checkup，或只用 checkup 這個字。而「去看醫生以進行健康檢查」就說成 go see a doctor for a checkup。
⓮ 「集資出錢」也可說成 contribute some money。

15 我用網路傳送賀電。

I use the Internet to send a congratulatory telegram.

16 我在我下屬的結婚典禮上致賀詞。

I make a congratulatory speech at my staff member's wedding.

17 客戶的父親過世了，所以我安排發唁電。

The client's father has passed away, so I arrange for a condolence telegram to be sent.

18 我為喪禮準備了慰問金。

I prepare condolence money for the funeral.

⓯ congratulatory 是「祝賀的」之意，而動詞的「祝賀」是 congratulate。
若用名詞的複數形 Congratulations! 則是表示「恭喜！」。

⓰ make a speech（致詞）也可說成 <u>deliver/give</u> a speech。

⓱ pass away（去世）是比 die（死掉）委婉有禮的說法。而 condolence
則是「慰問；哀悼」之意。

1 我希望能爭取到大客戶並獲得獎勵。
I'd like to get a big client and receive an award.

2 總裁的致詞一如往常不停重複，沒完沒了。
The president's speech is repetitive and goes on and on as usual.

3 等這個案子告一段落，我們大家一起去喝一杯，好好地開心一下！
When this project settles down, let's all go drinking and have some fun!

4 大家的時間總是很難配合。
It's difficult for everyone to agree on the schedule.

5 我就是不想坐在主任的旁邊！
I just don't want to sit next to the director!

6 史考特先生正在找老闆的麻煩。他實在不該忽略了身分地位和禮貌。
Mr. Scott is picking fights with the boss. He shouldn't ignore rank and manners.

big client ＝ 大客戶／receive an award ＝ 獲得獎勵

「我的夢想是獲得獎勵」可說成 It's my dream to receive an award.。而「得獎是莫大的光榮」則可說成 It is a great honor to receive the award.。

---

repetitive ＝ 重複的；反覆的／go on and on ＝ 不斷延續；沒完沒了／as usual ＝ 一如往常地

「致詞；發表演說」可說成 make/deliver/give a speech，而「即席演說」可用 give a speech on the spot，至於「簡潔的演說」則是 short/brief speech。

---

settle down ＝ 告一段落；穩定下來／go drinking ＝ 去喝一杯／have fun ＝ 開心享樂

「讓我們去狂歡吧！」可說成 Let's go out and party!。

It's difficult for ～ to ... ＝ 對～來說…是很困難的／agree on ～ ＝ 針對～達成一致的意見

「我的行程滿檔」就說成 My schedule is full.，而「我調整（變更）我的行程」則說成 I adjust (change) my schedule.。

---

just ＝ 就是～；只是～／next to ～ ＝ ～的旁邊／director ＝ 主任

此例句也可說成 I just want to avoid sitting next to the director!（我只想避免坐在主任的旁邊！）。

---

pick fights with ～ ＝ 找～的麻煩；挑釁～／ignore ＝ 忽視；不顧

「對～不禮貌」可說成 be rude to～，e.g. He was rude to the boss.（他對老板不禮貌）。

7 他喝醉以後真是判若兩人。
He's totally different once he gets drunk.

8 萬歲！我在賓果遊戲中贏到一張旅遊優惠券！
Hooray! I won a travel coupon at the bingo game!

9 非常感謝你為我做的一切。
Thank you very much for everything you have done for me.

10 你離開之後我會想念你的。祝你幸運，並在新的工作崗位上繼續做好你的工作。
I'll miss you when you're gone. I wish you good luck, and keep up the good work at your new workplace.

11 我不知道能不能熬過所有的尾牙活動。
I don't know if I can survive all these year-end parties.

12 去年尾牙我因為喝得爛醉而搞砸了，所以我今年要試著低調一些，保持清醒。
I got totally drunk and screwed up at the last year-end party, so I'll try to lay low and stay sober this year.

totally = 完全地;徹底地／once ~ = 一旦～／get drunk = 喝醉;酒醉

此例句也可說成 He changes a lot when he gets drunk.（他喝醉以後就變了一個人）。

Hooray! = 萬歲!（發音為 [hʊˋre]）／won = 贏得了;獲得了（為 win 的過去式和過去分詞）／travel coupon = 旅遊優惠券（coupon = 優惠券;折價券）

遊戲的「獎品」說成 prize,而「贏得獎品」就說成 win a prize。

---

for everything = 對於所有的事／you have done for me = 你為我做的

此例句也可說成 Thank you for all of your help.（感謝你的一切幫助）。

---

miss = 想念～／wish ~ good luck = 祝～幸運／keep up the good work = 繼續做好工作;維持良好的工作表現（keep up = 繼續做）／workplace = 職場;工作崗位

「祝你幸運」也可以簡單地用 Good luck! 表達。

I don't know if ~ = 我不知能否～／survive = 生存下去;熬過去／year-end party = 尾牙（也可用 end-of-the-year party）

此例句也可說成 I have so many year-end parties that I don't know if I can make it.（我有這麼多場尾牙要參加,不知我是否都能辦到）。

---

get drunk = 喝醉／screw up = 搞砸;出糗／lay low = 低調行事;保持安靜／stay sober = 保持清醒

「醉漢」說成 a drunk,而「我酒醒了」則可說成 I sobered up.。

13 尾牙時我該做什麼表演？真令人頭痛。

What kind of party trick should I do for the year-end party? It's a pain in the neck.

14 王先生看似含蓄安靜，所以我從沒想到他在宴會上竟然能這麼有趣。

Mr. Wang seems reserved and very quiet, so I never guessed he'd be so entertaining at a party.

15 要是他在工作上也能像在宴會上那麼積極熱情就好了。

I wish he would work on his job as enthusiastically as he acts at parties.

16 讓我們鼓掌為宴會畫上句點吧！

Let's wrap up the party by clapping our hands!

17 我聽說這次公司將舉辦部門對抗保齡球大賽。

I hear the company will hold an inter-division bowling tournament.

18 你可以選擇是否參加保齡球賽；這並不是強制性的。

It's up to you whether you take part in the bowling tournament; it's not obligatory.

what kind of = 什麼樣的;什麼種類的／party trick = 宴會表演（trick = 戲法；把戲）／a pain in the neck = 惱人的事（neck = 脖子）

「令人頭痛;令人傷透腦筋」也可說成 It gives me a headache.（這真令我頭痛）。

---

reserved = 含蓄的／quiet = 安靜的／I never guessed ~ = 我從沒想到～／he'd be so ~ = 他竟然能如此～（'d = would）／entertaining = 有趣的;使人愉快的 cf. entertain = 使歡樂;娛樂～

專業的「藝人」說成 entertainer。

I wish ~ = 我希望～;要是～就好了／as ~ as ... = 和…一樣地～／enthusiastically = 積極熱情地

注意，wish 之後的動詞或助動詞必須用過去式，如本例中的 would。

---

wrap up = 結束;總結／clap hands = 鼓掌

「為～熱烈鼓掌」說成 give~a big hand，e.g. Let's give him a big hand.（讓我們為他熱烈鼓掌）。

I hear ~ = 我聽說～／hold = 舉辦;舉行／inter-division = 各部門彼此間的（inter-~ = ~間的）／tournament = 錦標賽;比賽

「大賽將於下週舉行」可說成 The tournament will be held next week.。

It's up to you = 由你決定／whether ~ = 是否要～／take part in ~ = 參加～／obligatory = 強制的;義務的

「去打保齡球」說成 go bowling，而「保齡球場」則叫 bowling alley。

19 缺乏團隊合作我們是無法贏得比賽的。
We cannot win the tournament without teamwork.

20 好球！
Great shot!

21 我負責安排今年公司的員工旅遊。
I'm responsible for organizing the company trip this year.

22 同事結婚我該包多少錢？
How much money should I give as a gift for my colleague's wedding?

23 我必須參加好多場婚宴，要拿出這麼多禮金來可真傷荷包。
I have to attend a lot of wedding receptions, and it's expensive to come up with all that gift money.

24 我的定期健康檢查即將來臨。我希望今年我一切正常。
My regular health checkup is coming up. I hope nothing is wrong with me this year.

win the tournament = 贏得比賽／without ~ = 少了～；缺乏～
「團隊合作是勝利的關鍵」可說成 Teamwork is the key to victory.。

---

shot = 投、擊、踢球
great shot 也可用 <u>nice/beautiful</u> shot 等來替代。

---

be responsibility for ~ = 負責～／company trip = 員工旅遊
本例句中的 organizing 可用 arranging 代替。

---

give ~ as a gift = 送～做為禮物／wedding = 婚禮 cf. wedding present = 結婚賀禮
在歐美國家，結婚是不送禮金的，一般會事先將該對新人想要的物品清單登錄至商店、百貨公司（bridal registry），然後由送禮的人依自己的預算選擇合適商品來贈送。

---

attend = 參加；出席／wedding reception = 結婚喜宴／expensive = 貴的；花錢的／come up with ~ = 拿出～／gift money = 禮金
「我受邀參加婚宴」就說成 I was invited to the wedding reception.。

---

regular = 定期的／health checkup = 健康檢查（「健康檢查」也可用 <u>physical/medical</u> checkup 等說法）／come up = 接近；即將到來／nothing is wrong with ~ = ～一切都好
「我定期接受健康檢查」就說成 I have a health checkup regularly.。

25 我很擔心我的腰圍。
I'm worried about my waistline.

26 喔，不！我的視力又變差了！
Oh, no! My eyesight got worse again!

27 知道健康檢查的結果讓我鬆了一口氣。
I'm relieved to know the results of my medical checkup.

be worried about ~ = 擔心~；憂慮~／waistline = 腰圍
「過重」説成 overweight；「肥胖」説成 obese。

---

eyesight = 視力 e.g. have <u>good</u> (<u>bad</u>) eyesight = 視力好（差）／get worse
= 惡化（worse 是 bad（壞）的比較級）
「你不戴眼鏡時的視力如何？」就説成 What's your eyesight like without your
glasses on?。

---

be relieved = 鬆一口氣／result of ~ = ～的結果／medical checkup = 健康檢
查
本例也可説成 It's a relief to know that I'm healthy.（知道我很健康讓我鬆了一
口氣），句中的 relief 則為名詞。

Skit  公司活動篇 ——————————————

要花錢又要費心，公司內的交際可不輕鬆呢！

Man: **Did you go to the department lunch party? I didn't see you.**

Woman: **No, I had to organize the farewell party for Jenny.**

M: **It was fun. I made a toast that everyone enjoyed.**

W: **Did you have to pour the manager's beer?**

M: **Yes, but he's totally different once he gets drunk. He was very funny.**

W: **I'm sorry I missed❶ it. Hey, are you going to attend Jeremy's wedding reception?**

M: **Yes, and thanks for reminding❷❸ me. I have to pick up an envelope for his gift money.**

W: **How much money should I give?**

M: **I think NT3,600 will be enough❹. His❺ wlll be the third company wedding this year. It's expensive coming up with all that gift money.**

W: **I have to make a congratulatory speech at the wedding but I don't know him that well.**

M: **Let's have lunch together. I'll help❻ you write it.**

W: **Thanks!**

男性：妳有參加部門的中午聚餐嗎？我沒看到妳。

女性：我沒去，我得替珍妮安排歡送會。

男：很好玩呢。我敬了酒，而大家都很開心。

女：你必須替經理倒啤酒嗎？

男：是啊，不過他喝醉以後真是判若兩人。他超好笑的。

女：真可惜我沒看到。對了，你會參加傑若米的婚宴嗎？

男：會，謝謝妳提醒了我。我得去找個紅包袋來包他的禮金。

女：我該包多少呢？

男：我想三千六應該很夠了。他的婚宴是今年公司裡的第三場了。要拿出這麼多禮金來可真傷荷包。

女：我必須在婚禮上致賀詞，但是我並不是那麼了解他。

男：我們一起去吃午飯吧。我會幫忙妳寫祝賀詞。

女：多謝！

【單字片語】

❶ miss：錯過

❷ thanks for ~ing：謝謝你替我做～

❸ remind：提醒～

❹ enough：足夠的

❺ his：= his wedding

❻ help ~ ...：幫忙～做…

Quick Check

讓我們一起來複習本章所介紹過的句型！請依據以下中文句子的意思，完成對應的英文句子。（答案就在本頁最下方）

❶ 我發表新年演說。 →P212

I ( ) the New Year's ( ).

❷ 我在網路上尋找舉辦歡送會用的餐廳。 →P213

I look for a restaurant for the ( ) ( ) on the Internet.

❸ 我參加公司的高爾夫球賽。 →P213

I ( ) the company golf ( ).

❹ 我接受在職訓練。 →P214

I receive ( ) ( ).

❺ 等這個案子告一段落，我們大家一起去喝一杯，好好地開心一下！ →P216

When this project ( ) ( ), let's all go drinking and have some ( )!

❻ 大家的時間總是很難配合。 →P216

It's difficult for everyone to ( ) ( ) ( ) ( ).

❼ 史考特先生正在找老闆的麻煩。他實在不該忽略了身分地位和禮貌。 →P216

Mr. Scott is ( ) ( ) with the boss. He shouldn't ignore ( ) and ( ).

❽ 我不知能不能熬過所有的尾牙活動。 →P218

I don't ( ) ( ) I can ( ) all these year-end parties.

❾ 尾牙時我該做什麼表演？真令人頭痛。 →P220

What kind of party ( ) should I do for the year-end party? It's a ( ) ( ) ( ) ( ).

❿ 你可以選擇是否參加保齡球賽；這並不是強制性的。 →P220

It's ( ) ( ) ( ) whether you ( ) ( ) ( ) the bowling ( ); it's not ( ).

---

❶give/speech ❷farewell/party ❸enter/ competition ❹on-the-job/training ❺ settles/ down/fun ❻agree/on/the/schedule ❼picking/fights/rank/manners ❽know/if/ survive ❾trick/pain/in/the/neck ❿up/to/ you/take/part/in/tournament/obligatory

chapter 9

人事、待遇
Personnel Matters

本章收集了僱用形式、人事考核、薪資、職務異動…等等，各式各樣與工作環境相關的句型及表達方式。

由於這些對員工來說都是重大問題，

談到時心中免不了五味雜陳，

而喜怒哀樂交替的各種心聲想必也會隨之增加。

Words 單字篇

❶正職、正式員工

❻人事部門

❷臨時僱員；派遣員工
❸人力派遣公司
❹臨時工
❺招募

❼人事考核
❽自我考核
❾業績
❿實力主義

⓫年假
⓬退休

⓭產假；育嬰假

⓮病假

⓯工作環境

❶permanent employee ❷temp staff ❸temporary-employment agency ❹temporary worker ❺recruitment ❻personnel department ❼personnel evaluation ❽self-evaluation ❾business performance ❿ability-based system ⓫annual paid holidays ⓬retirement

首先，讓我們透過各種事、物的名稱，
來掌握「人事、待遇」給人的整體印象。

⑲升遷
⑳降職
㉑無休止的
　激烈競手

㉒加薪
㉓減薪

⑯薪資
⑰獎金
⑱年薪制

㉔辭職信

㉕提早退休
㉖終身僱用

⑬maternity leave　⑭medical leave　⑮working environment
⑯pay　⑰bonus　⑱annual salary system　⑲promotion　⑳demotion
㉑rat race　㉒pay raise　㉓pay cut　㉔letter of resignation　㉕early
retirement　㉖permanent employment

1 我打工。
I work part-time.

2 我工作時間較短。
I work shorter hours.

3 我每週有三天在家工作。
I work at home three days a week.

4 我去人力派遣公司登記。
I sign up with a temporary-employment agency.

5 我被派遣到一家公司。
I am dispatched to a company.

tips

❶ 此例句也可改用 work on a part-time basis、work as a part-timer 等說法。
❸ 「〔利用電話或網路〕在家工作」說成 do telecommuting。
❹ 「人力派遣公司」也可說成 staffing company。
❻ I terminate my contract with the company. 就是「我和該公司解約」。

6 我每年更新一次我的派遣合約。
I renew my temporary contract every year.

7 我和同事一同分擔工作。
I share the workload with colleagues.

8 我退休後以臨時工的身分繼續留下來工作。
I continue to work as a temporary worker after retirement.

9 我以彈性工時工作。
I work flextime.

Mon | Tue | Wed | Th | Fr

10 我週休二日。
I have two days off every week.

❽ 「在某個固定期間，和正職員工一樣地工作的臨時工」就是 temporary worker，而「只在特定日期、時間工作的人」則是 part-time worker。

❾ 此例句也可改用 work a flexible schedule/flexible hours 這樣的說法。

❿ 「我們公司採取週休二日制」可說成 My company has a five-day workweek system.。

11 我上午請假。
I take the morning off.

12 我把我的有薪休假（年假）全部用完。
I use all my <u>paid days off</u> (<u>annual paid holidays</u>).

13 我請產假（育嬰假）。
I take maternity leave.

14 我加班。
I work <u>overtime/ after hours</u>.

15 我向上司申請加班。
I apply for permission from my boss to work overtime.

tips

⓬ I'm on a paid holiday today. 就是「我今天放有薪假」。

⓭ 「產假」和「育嬰假」都可用 maternity leave表示。若是男性請「育嬰假」，則可用 paternity leave（陪產假）。而「產假（育嬰假）後重返工作崗位」可說成 return to work after taking maternity leave。

16 我假日來上班。
I come to work on a holiday.

17 我要求改善我們的工作環境。
I request improvements in our working environment.

18 我與人事部門面談。
I have an interview with the personnel department.

19 我獲得升遷（加薪）。
I get a promotion (pay raise).

⑭ 一般來說，overtime 是指「有加班費的超時工作」，而 after hours 則是所謂的「無薪加班」。

⑮ cut back on unnecessary overtime 就是「減少不必要的加班」。

⑱ 「握有人事掌控權」可說成 have the power to shuffle personnel。

⑲ 相反地，「遭到降職」說成 suffer a demotion，而「被減薪」則是 take a pay cut。

20 我對我的考核結果提出質疑。
I question my evaluation.

21 我收到有關自我考核的回饋意見。
I receive feedback about the self-evaluation.

22 我申請調動。
I request a transfer.

23 我從九月一日起將轉調到業務部。
I'll be transferred to the sales department as of September 1.

24 我暫時在公司的關係企業工作。
I work temporarily at an affiliate company.

tips

⑳ 「對～覺得滿意」可説成 be happy with ～，e.g. I'm happy with my evaluation.（我對我的考績很滿意）。
㉑ 「自我考核表」可用 self-evaluation form。
㉒ 「辭職信」就説成 letter of resignation，e.g. I submitted a letter of resignation.（我送出了辭職信）。

25 我轉調到新的職場，並對那邊的員工進行了禮貌性的訪問。
I'm transferred to a new workplace, and make courtesy visits to the staff there.

26 我把和我處不好的員工送走。
I send off <u>an employee/a worker</u> I don't get along with.

27 我受到提早退休的壓力。
I'm pressured into early retirement.

28 我獲選成為小組組長。
I'm selected as team leader.

㉔ 「子公司」可說成 subsidiary company。
㉕ 「進行禮貌性的訪問」也可說成 go the rounds of courtesy calls。
㉖ get along with 指「相處融洽」。另，「解雇」為 lay off。
㉗ 「冗員」可用 deadwood employee 來表達。

1 我的個性真的適合做派遣員工。
I sure have a bent for temping.

2 她是派遣員工，但她工作起來可能比正式員工還努力。
She's a temp but she might work more than a permanent employee.

3 夠了！我無法在差勁的主管之下工作。
That's it. I can't work under a lousy boss.

4 簽約時的說明似乎和實際職務內容不符。
The explanation at the time of the contract signing doesn't seem to conform to the actual job duties.

5 不知那位派遣員工是否想成為我們的全職員工。
I wonder if that temp wants to join us full-time.

6 近來，連正式員工都無法對終身僱用感到安心。
Even permanent employees don't feel assured of permanent employment these days.

have a bent for ～ = 個性適合～；適合做～／temp（= work as a temporary worker）= 做派遣員工；做臨時僱員

「個性不適合～；不適合做～」則用 not cut out for ～，e.g. I don't think I'm cut out for accounting.（我不覺得我適合做會計）。

---

temp = 派遣員工；臨時僱員（temp = temporary worker）／permanent employee = 正式員工

「兼職、打工者」稱為 part-timer，e.g. The company needs to hire more part-timers.（公司需要多僱用幾個兼職人員）。另，「全職人員」則為 full-timer。

---

work under ～ = 在～之下工作／lousy = 差勁的；糟糕的

lousy 也可用來修飾事物，e.g. a lousy system（一個很爛的制度）。

---

seem to ～ = 似乎～／conform to ～ = 和～一致／job duties = 工作職責；職務內容

That's totally different from what I heard! 就是「那跟我聽到的完全不一樣！」。另外，「內容」可用 content 表示，如「職務內容」就說成 job content，而「業務內容」便是 business content。

I wonder if ～ = 不知是否～／join = 加入～（這裡的 us 是指公司）／full-time = 全職的（地）

「提拔～」可用 promote 這個字，e.g. We're actively promoting women in the sales department.（敝公司的業務部現在正積極提拔女性員工）。

---

feel assured of ～ = 對～感到安心／permanent employment = 終身僱用

「就業不安全」就說成 employment insecurity，e.g. Have you ever felt stressed about employment insecurity?（你是否也曾感受到就業不安全的壓力？）。

7　我們今年不做大規模的招募。
We won't do any mass recruitment this year.

8　有連續假期我當然很高興，但悲哀的是，像我這種計時人員，休假時是沒有錢拿的。
Of course I'm happy with consecutive holidays, but, sadly enough, an hourly-wage worker like me doesn't get paid for them.

9　今天是發薪日。我好期待這一天。
Today is payday. I've really been looking forward to it.

10　喔，補充一下，那不是稅後的，而是稅前的。
Oh, that's not after-tax but before-tax, I might add.

11　知道自己的薪水被扣了這麼多稅，實在很令人沮喪。
It's so frustrating just to know this much tax is deducted from my paycheck.

12　由於經濟持續不景氣所以每個員工都將減薪 5%。這真荒謬！
Every employee's going to have their salary cut by 5 percent because of the on-going recession. This is ridiculous!

mass recruitment＝大規模的招募（mass＝大規模的）

「畢業生招募；校園徵才」說成 graduate recruitment，而「〔針對在職人士的〕轉職招募」則說成 mid-career recruitment。

---

consecutive holidays＝連假／sadly enough＝悲哀的是／hourly-wage＝以時薪計酬的／get paid for ～＝因～獲得酬勞

get paid by the hour 就是「依工時計薪；拿時薪」，e.g. Students get paid by the hour at NT120.（學生是時薪 120 元）。

---

payday＝發薪日／look forward to ～＝期待～

I can hardly wait for payday. 就是「發薪日怎麼還沒到，我快等不及了」。另外，由於美金鈔票上印有老鷹圖案，所以美國的發薪日還可用俚語 when the eagle flies 來表達。

---

after-tax＝扣稅之後的／before-tax＝扣稅之前的

I might add 就是「讓我補充一下～」之意，用於陳述附加資訊的時候。「所得稅」是 income tax，而「扣稅後的薪資（實得薪資）」則用 take-home（可拿回家的東西）來表達。

---

frustrating＝令人沮喪的；令人洩氣的／this much ～＝這麼多的～／be deducted from ～＝從～被扣掉／paycheck＝薪資；支付薪水的支票

「自動扣除」可用 be automatically deducted 來表達，e.g. Income tax is automatically deducted from pay.（所得稅會從薪資中自動扣除）。

---

have ～ cut＝將～減少／on-going＝目前持續進行的／recession＝經濟不景氣

可用來表達經濟不景氣之意的字還有 depression（蕭條）、downturn（衰退）、slowdown（趨緩）等。

13 我的工作報酬就只有這樣？我所做的顯然有比這更高的價值！
Is this all I get for my job? Obviously, what I do is worth more than this!

14 既然薪水減少了，或許我該開始兼差了。
Maybe I should start moonlighting, since my salary was reduced.

15 用我的第一筆獎金買些東西給家鄉的父母如何？
How about buying something for my parents back home with my first bonus?

16 除非情況好轉，否則我們應該領不到多少冬季獎金。
Unless things turn around, we won't get much of a winter bonus.

17 從好的方面來看，這種時局我竟然還能領到獎金呢。
The good thing is that I get to receive a bonus at a time like this.

18 你知道嗎？我們會領到一筆特別獎金，因為我們的業績提升了。
You know what? We'll get a special bonus because our business performance has improved.

Obviously, ~ = 顯然，～／worth more than ~ = 價值超過～

「這工作不划算」可說成 This job doesn't pay.，而其中的 pay 是「有利；值得；划算」之意。另外，注意本例第二句中的 worth「值」為介系詞，其後接名詞、代名詞或動名詞，e.g. This book is worth reading.（這本書值得一讀）。

moonlight = 兼差／reduce = 減少；降低

moonlight 做為動詞使用時，有「〔在晚上以副業形式〕兼做其他工作」的意思。這是從在月光下偷偷工作的形象衍伸而來的說法。

How about ~ing? = 做～如何？／back home = 家鄉的；老家的

「拿到獎金」可說成 get/receive a bonus，e.g. I got a big bonus this year.（我今年拿到一大筆獎金）、We receive a bonus twice a year.（我們一年領兩次獎金）。

unless ~ = 除非～／things = 情況／turn around = 好轉

turn around 的名詞形為 turnaround，有「好轉；由虧轉盈」等意思。e.g. We've achieved a turnaround this year.（我們公司今年成功地由虧轉盈）。

get to ~ = 有能夠～的機會

The good thing is [that] ~ 就是「好的一面是～」的意思。而類似的句型還有 The thing is ~（重點是～；問題在於～），e.g. The thing is we can't move on to the next stage.（問題是，我們無法進入下一階段）。

You know what? = 你知道嗎？（用來喚起對方注意力的說法）／performance = 表現；績效／improve = 改善；提升

其他可用來喚起對方注意力的說法還有：談論有趣話題時用的 Guess what.（你猜怎樣）、針對對方行動給予建議時用的 Tell you what.（我跟你說）等。

19 我的薪水只夠付貸款和生活費。
My salary is only enough to pay the loans and living expenses.

20 我們公司採年薪制。
Our company adopts the annual salary system.

21 經理是沒有加班費的。
Managers don't get paid for overtime work.

22 太棒了！今天是無加班日。
Hooray! It's a no-overtime day today.

23 我想我會把剩下的有薪假合併起來，放個長假。
I think I'm going to make it a long vacation by combining all the unused paid holidays.

24 我打算用完我的有薪假。
I plan to use up my paid holidays.

living expenses = 生活費

具代表性的 expenses（費用）包括：food expenses（飲食費）、traffic expenses（交通費）、medical expenses（醫藥費）、educational expenses（教育費）、entertainment expenses（娛樂開支）等。

---

adopt = 採取／annual = 每年的；一年一次的

此例句也可説成 We are paid on an annual basis in the company.，其中 on ~ basis 就是「以～方式」，e.g. I write e-mail in English on a daily basis.（我每天寫英文電子郵件）。

---

manager = 經理／get paid for ~ = 因～獲得酬勞／overtime work = 加班

「加班費」是 overtime premium，而「無薪加班」可説成 unpaid overtime。

---

no-overtime = 不加班的

「準時下班」可説成 leave the office on time，e.g. Why don't we leave the office on time and go have a drink?（我們何不準時下班，然後去喝一杯？）

---

combine = 合併／unused = 尚未使用的

vacation 指「較長的假期」，e.g. summer vacation（暑假）、winter vacation（寒假）。

---

use up~ = 把～用完

「〔把有薪休假〕展延〔至下一年度〕」可用 carry over ~，e.g. I don't know how many paid holidays I can carry over.（我不知我能把多少天的有薪休假展延至下一年度）。

25 你要有醫師診斷證明才能申請病假。
You need a doctor's certificate to apply for medical leave.

---

26 我痛恨把生命全用在工作上。我重視工作和生活的平衡。
I hate to spend my life working all the time. I value the balance of work and life.

---

27 聽說現在在馬布利公司請產假還是會被擺臉色。
They say taking maternity leave is still frowned upon at Marbley.

---

28 近來有越來越多男人請陪產假。時代真的不一樣了。
More and more men are taking paternity leave these days. It's a whole different world.

---

29 我明天開始休產假。我希望這不會造成你的不便。
I'm going on maternity leave tomorrow. I hope it won't cause you any inconvenience.

---

30 終身僱用制已成為歷史。現今，實力主義正日漸普及。
Permanent employment is already a thing of the past. Nowadays, ability-based systems have become widespread.

doctor's certificate = 醫師診斷證明／medical leave = 病假

apply for ~ 就是「申請~」的意思，e.g. apply for <u>unemployment benefits</u> (<u>a</u> <u>tax deduction</u>)（申請失業給付（稅金減免））。「申請」有時也可用 claim （要求）這個動詞，例如 claim workers' compensation（申請職業災害賠償）。

hate to ~ = 痛恨~／value = 重視

有句相關諺語説成 All work and no play makes Jack a dull boy.（只工作不玩耍，聰明小孩也變傻）。而「工作狂」則説成 workaholic [ˌwɜkəˋhalɪk]。

they say = 他們説（聽説）／maternity leave = 產假；育嬰假／be frowned upon = 被擺臉色；遭白眼（frown = 皺眉）

frown upon 指「對~表示不悦」，e.g. The boss frowned upon his secretary's attitude.（老板對他秘書的態度表示不悦）。

more and more ~ = 越來越多~／paternity leave = 陪產假／whole different = 完全不同的

paternity 是「父親身分」之意，故 paternity leave 就是「〔由父親申請的〕陪產假、育嬰假」。

go on ~ = 開始休~／cause you ~ = 造成你~；導致你~／inconvenience = 不方便

inconvenience 可做為動詞使用，表達「對~造成不便」之意，e.g. I hope I didn't inconvenience you in my absence.（我希望我的缺席沒有對你造成不便）。

permanent employment = 終身僱用／a thing of the past = 過去的東西／ability-based = 以能力為基礎的／widespread = 普遍的；流行的

「年資制度」可説成 seniority system，e.g. Japanese companies are gradually phasing out the seniority system.（日本公司正在逐步廢止年資制度），其中的 phase out 指「逐步廢止；漸漸廢除」。

31 考核的依據是如此地含糊曖昧，我無法認同。
The basis for the evaluation is so vague I can't go along with it.

32 他在人事考核上是不是有點太寬鬆了？我很好奇他考量的到底是哪部分。
Isn't he a bit too lenient in personnel evaluations? I wonder what he takes into account.

33 她對自己的評價很高。
She thinks highly of herself.

34 別一次攬下這麼多工作。你應該把一些工作交給你的員工。
Don't take a lot of tasks at once. You should leave some of them to your staff.

35 可以請您給我更多業務員做的工作嗎？
Could you give me more jobs as a salesperson?

36 憂鬱症已然成為一種常見疾病。
Depression sure has become a disease that's close to home.

basis for ～ = ～的根據／vague = 模糊的／go along with ～ = 贊同～

欲詢問對方發言的「依據」時，可用 What do you base that on?（你的依據是什麼？）、On what grounds do you say that?（你是依據什麼基礎所以這麼說？）等說法。

---

a bit too ～ = 有點太～／lenient = 寬鬆的；仁慈的／personnel evaluation = 人事考核／take ～ into account = 將～納入考量

「寬鬆的評分者」說成 <u>lenient/generous</u> grader。

---

think highly of ～ = 對～有高評價

「老闆對她讚嘆不已」說成 The boss speaks highly of her.。

---

at once = 一次；同時／leave ～ to ... = 把～交給…

「把工作分配給～」可用 assign a job to ～ 這種說法。另外，「我和同事一同分擔工作」可說成 I share my workload with my colleagues.。而 work-sharing（分攤工作）也是相當廣為人知的用詞，e.g. We've adopted a work-sharing system.（我們公司已採用工作分攤制度）。

---

as ～ = 做為～／salesperson = 業務員

「這個工作不適合我」說成 This job isn't suitable for me.。

---

depression = 憂鬱症／disease = 疾病／be close to home = 常見的；熟悉的

close to home 原意是「離家近的」，亦即「自己熟悉的」之意。另外，close to home 也可指「正中要害」，e.g. His remark was so close to home that I couldn't say a word.（他的話正中要害，使我說不出話來）。

37 他是同輩中最有前途的一個。
He's the most up-and-coming among my peers.

38 只要我在這個部門工作,升官的可能性就微乎其微。
As long as I work here in this department, the chances are slim that I'll get a promotion.

39 我真的很想遠離這永無止盡的激烈競爭。
I really want to stay out of the rat race.

40 我已經在這個部門做了很久,我想轉調到不同地方開闢一些新的可能性。
I've been working in the department for so long I want to transfer to somewhere different to open up some new possibilities.

41 這算是升官還是降職?
Is this a promotion or a demotion?

42 我聽說,明年春天經理可望升官並轉調至總公司。
From what I heard, the manager is expected to be promoted and transferred to the main office next spring.

up-and-coming = 很有發展的；有前途的／peer = 同輩；同儕

「有前途的」也可用 promising 來表達，e.g. She's a promising young artist.（她是個有前途的年輕藝術家）。

---

as long as ~ = 只要～／chances are slim that ~ = ～的機會渺茫／get a promotion = 獲得升遷

chances 有「可能性」的意思，而 Chances are that ~（很可能～）是會話中一種常見的表達方式，e.g. Chances are that the guy will be transferred.（那傢伙很可能會被調走）。

---

stay out of ~ = 對～置身事外／rat race = 永無止盡的激烈競爭

「成功者忙碌的生活方式」可說成 fast lane，e.g. Josh's trying hard to get into the fast lane.（賈許努力地想擠進成功者之林）。

---

transfer to ~ = 轉調至～／open up = 開闢；開拓／possibility = 可能性

「〔人的〕潛在能力」就說成 one's potential，e.g. I need to fully exert my potential to tackle the difficult task.（我需要充分發揮自己的潛能，以應付那個艱難的任務）。

---

promotion = 升遷；升官／demotion = 降職；降級

be <u>promoted</u>/<u>demoted</u> to ~ 就是「被晉升／降級至～」，e.g. Mr. Hemans was <u>promoted</u>/<u>demoted</u> to assistant manager.（海曼斯先生被晉升／降級為協理）。另外還有 get a promotion（獲得升遷）、suffer a demotion（遭到降職）等說法。

---

from what I head = 依據我聽到的／be expected to ~ = 可望～；預計將～／main office = 總公司

「透過小道消息聽說～」可說成 hear ~ <u>through</u>/<u>on</u> the grapevine，其中的 grapevine 原指「葡萄藤」，在此衍申成「口耳相傳」之意，e.g. I heard this <u>through</u>/<u>on</u> the grapevine — she's getting married.（我透過小道消息聽說一她要結婚了）。

43 這真是個出乎意料的人事異動。
This sure is an out-of-the-blue transfer.

44 在我買了新房子之後，就被調到了分公司。
I got transferred to the branch office right after purchasing a new home.

45 我想我別無選擇，只能隻身離家到遠地工作。
I guess I have no choice but to live away from home for work.

46 由於被公司轉調至他處，我將被迫與女朋友維持遠距離的戀愛關係。
Because of the company transfer I got, I'm going to have to have a long-distance relationship with my girlfriend.

47 我將轉調到一個完全不同領域的部門去。
I'm going to transfer to a department out of my field.

48 說真的，只有馬屁精能出人頭地。
Seriously, only brown-nosers can move up the ladder.

out-of-the-blue = 意外的;出乎意料的/transfer = 調動;調職

「晴天霹靂」說成 a bolt out of the blue（藍天中 <blue sky> 突如其來的閃電 <thunderbolt>），e.g. The news that she got pregnant was a real bolt out of the blue.（她懷孕的消息可真是晴天霹靂）。

got transferred = 被調職/right after ~ = 就在～之後/purchase = 購買

「我毫無怨言地接受了調職」說成 I accept the company transfer without complaining.、「我為了家人而拒絕調職」說成 I decline the transfer for the sake of my family.。

have no choice but to ~ = 沒有其他選擇,只能～/live away from home for work = 為工作隻身離家生活

英文裡沒有相當於「單身外派」的說法,故須以 live away from home for work（為了工作而離開家庭單獨生活）的方式來說明。

long-distance = 遠距離的/relation = 關係

「遠距離戀愛」也可直譯為 long-distance love,e.g. We can't see each other often because of our long-distance love.（由於是遠距離戀愛,所以我們無法常見面）。

out of one's field = 和自己完全不同領域的

「格格不入的人」可用魚來譬喻,說成 fish out of water（離開水的魚）。e.g. I've been feeling like a fish out of water in this department.（在這個部門裡,我一直感覺自己格格不入）。

Seriously, ~ = 說真的,～/brown-noser = 馬屁精/move up the ladder = 往上爬;出人頭地

「馬屁精」也可用 apple-polisher 表示。

49 我很擔心不知道自己在暫時被派遣的工作職場上是否會受到歡迎。

I'm concerned whether I'll be welcome at the new workplace where I'm going to be working temporarily.

50 我想我應該替接手我工作的人準備一些資料。

I think I should prepare some materials for the person taking over my job.

51 我聽說他試圖偷偷地換工作。

I heard that he's trying to switch companies on the sly.

52 我很好奇，像他這種工作狂，退休以後要做什麼。

I wonder what he's going to do after retirement; he's such a workaholic.

53 部門內部公布了業務轉換命令。

A switch of job duties was announced in the department.

54 自從我的上司變成美國人後，我便有機會改變工作步調。

I get to vary the pace of my work performance since an American became my boss.

be concerned whether ~ = 擔心是否～／temporaily = 暫時地

本句中 I'm concerned 可用 I'm worried about 代替。

---

material = 資料／take over ~ = 接手～；接管～

「A 是 B 的繼任者」也可用 B be replaced by A 的說法來表達，e.g. Mr. Chen has been replaced by Mr. Yang.（楊先生已繼任了陳先生的職務）。

---

switch ~ = 換～／on the sly = 偷偷地；暗地裡

可表達「偷偷地；暗中」等意思的說法還包括 secretly（秘密地）、behind someone's back（背著某人）等。另外還有 like a thief in the night（像個在夜裡的小偷般）這種有趣的講法，e.g. He snuck out of the meeting like a thief in the night.（他偷偷摸摸地離開會議，就像個在夜裡的小偷般；snuck 是 sneak（偷偷溜走）的過去式和過去分詞）

---

retirement = 退休／workaholic = 工作狂

「屆齡退休」說成 age-limit/compulsory retirement。「退休後開始培養興趣」可說成 take up a hobby after retirement，而「退休後過著悠閒自在的生活」則可說成 bask in retirement，其中的 bask 原意為「曬太陽」，在此引申指「沉浸；享受」。

---

switch = 變更；轉換／announce = 宣佈／job duties = 業務；職務

job duties 是指「〔工作上的〕職責；職務；業務」等，e.g. My job duties are going to double my present responsibilities.（我的業務量將變成目前職務的兩倍之多）。另外「〔業務等的〕交接程序」就說成 handover process。

---

get to ~ = 有機會～／vary = 改變；變換／pace = 步調；節奏

「改變氣氛」可用 change the atmosphere 來表達，e.g. The new secretary completely changed the atmosphere of the office.（新來的秘書徹底改變了辦公室氣氛）。

這樣不合理！我對人事考核有異議！

Woman: **That's it. I can't work under my lousy boss any more.**

Man: **What's the problem?❶**

W: **I'm questioning my evaluation. The basis for it is so vague, I just can't agree with it.**

M: **Can't you talk to him about it?**

W: **I tried but his explanation doesn't make any sense❷. Also, I work overtime almost every day❸ but I never get a promotion.**

M: **These days, you should be glad❹ you have a job at all❺.**

W: **I know that, but I've been working in the department so long. I want to transfer to somewhere different to open up new possibilities.**

M: **Can you request a transfer?**

W: **I have an interview with the personnel department tomorrow.**

M: **What if❻ they won't give you a transfer❼?**

W: **Maybe I'll quit❽ and work part time. I could work shorter hours and spend more time with my family.**

女性：夠了。我再也無法在我那爛主管之下工作。

男性：出了什麼問題？

女：我對我的考核結果提出質疑。考核的依據是如此地模糊曖昧，我無法認同。

男：妳不能和他針對此事談一談嗎？

女：我試過了，但是他的解釋根本毫無道理可言。而且，我幾乎每天都加班，可是從來沒獲得升遷。

男：這年頭，能有個工作妳就該心懷感激了。

女：我知道，可是我已在這個部門做了很久，我想轉調到不同地方好開闢一些新的可能性。

男：妳可以申請調動嗎？

女：我明天要和人事部面談。

男：要是他們不讓你調動的話，妳要怎麼辦？

女：我可能會辭職做兼職工作。這樣我可以縮短工時，有更多時間陪家人。

【單字片語】

❶ What's the problem?：發生什麼問題？

❷ not make any sense：毫無道理；完全沒意義

❸ almost every day：幾乎每天

❹ you should be glad：你應該偷笑；你應該心懷感激

❺ at all：只要；光是（在肯定句中）

❻ What if ~?：如果～的話怎麼辦？

❼ give ~ a transfer：讓～調動

❽ quit：辭職

Quick Check

讓我們一起來複習本章所介紹過的句型！請依據以下中文句子的意思，完成對應的英文句子。（答案就在本頁最下方）

❶ 我去人力派遣公司登記。→P232

I ( ) ( ) with a temporary-employment agency.

❷ 我的個性真的適合做派遣員工。→P238

I sure have ( ) ( ) ( ) temping.

❸ 我明天開始休產假。我希望這不會造成你的不便。→P246

I'm going on ( ) ( ) tomorrow. I hope it won't ( )
you any ( ).

❹ 終身僱用制已成為歷史。現今，實力主義日漸普及。→P246

( ) employment is already a ( ) of ( ) ( ).
Nowadays, ( ) systems have become ( ).

❺ 他是同輩中最有前途的一個。→P250

He's the most ( ) among my peers.

❻ 只要我在這個部門工作，升官的可能性就微乎其微。→P250

( ) ( ) ( ) I work here in this department, the
( ) ( ) ( ) that I'll get a ( ).

❼ 我真的很想遠離這永無止盡的激烈競爭。→P250

I really want to ( ) ( ) ( ) the ( )
( ).

❽ 這真是個出乎意料的人事異動。→P252

This sure is an ( ) ( ).

❾ 說真的，只有馬屁精能出人頭地。→P252

Seriously, only ( ) can ( ) ( ) the ( ).

❿ 我很好奇，像他這種工作狂，退休以後要做什麼。→P254

I wonder what he's going to do after ( ); he's such a ( ).

---

❶sign/up ❷a/bent/for ❸maternity/leave/
cause/inconvenience ❹Permanent/thing/
the/past/ability-based/widespread ❺up-
and-coming ❻As/long/as/chances/are/
slim/promotion ❼stay/out/of/rat/race ❽
out-of-the-blue/transfer ❾brown-nosers/
move/up/ladder ❿retirement/workaholic

chapter 10

下班

After-Work Hours

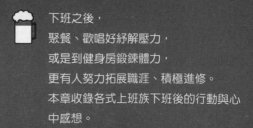

下班之後，
聚餐、歡唱好紓解壓力，
或是到健身房鍛鍊體力，
更有人努力拓展職涯、積極進修。
本章收錄各式上班族下班後的行動與心
中感想。

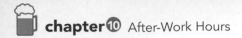

Words 單字篇

啤酒

❶飲酒聚會
❷居酒屋；小酒館

❸飲食攤
❹逛酒吧
❺宿醉

❾麥克風

❽卡拉 OK

❼網聚　❻聯誼

❿遙控器

❶drinking session ❷tavern ❸food stall ❹bar-hopping ❺hangover
❻mixer ❼off-line meeting ❽karaoke ❾microphone ❿remote
control ⓫cross-industrial exchange meeting ⓬study session
⓭seminar outside the company ⓮computer training school

首先，讓我們透過各種事、物的名稱，
來掌握「下班」給人的整體印象。

⑭電腦補習班　⑱副業
⑮日語班　　　⑲義工工作
⑯課程
⑰認證考試

⑳演唱會；音樂會
㉑戲劇

⑪跨產業
　交流會
⑫讀書會
⑬公司外的
　研討會

㉒美甲沙龍

㉖瑜珈教室

㉗健身房；運動俱樂部

㉓美容診所
㉔美容沙龍
㉕按摩院

⑮Japanese-language class　⑯lessons　⑰certification exam
⑱second job　⑲volunteer work　⑳concert　㉑play　㉒nail salon
㉓esthetic clinic　㉔beauty salon　㉕massage parlor　㉖yoga class
㉗gym

1 我邀請我同事去喝一杯。
I ask my colleague out for a drink.

2 我喝酒以忘卻煩惱。
I drink away my troubles.

3 我去大吃大喝。
I go on eating binges.

4 我去逛酒吧。
I go bar hopping.

5 我計畫了一個四男對四女的聯誼活動。
I set up a mixer for four men and four women.

tips

❶ ask ~ out 是「邀請～」之意，而 ask out for lunch 是「邀請人一同吃午餐」，ask out for a date 則是「邀請人去約會」。
❷ drink away~ 表達「用酒來忘卻～」之意。
❸ binge 是「盡情吃喝」的意思，而「暴飲暴食；飲食過量」則用 overeating。

6 我安排了同人數的男性與女性來聯誼。
I arrange the same number of men and women to come to the mixer.

7 我唱卡拉 OK 以紓解壓力。
I sing karaoke to release some stress.

8 我〔定期〕上健身房。
I go to the gym [regularly].

9 我跑步以彌補運動不足的問題。
I <u>run/jog</u> to make up for not getting enough exercise.

10 我在回家的路上租了片 DVD。
I rent a DVD on my way home.

❹ hopping 是「從一地接著往另一地不斷移動」之意。
❺ mixer 在美國用來指「男女混合的聯誼會」。
❼ Karaoke 就是「卡拉 OK」，但是請注意在英文中唸成 [ˌkærɪˋoki]。
❿ 此例句也可說成 I drop in the rental shop and rent a DVD on the way home. 。

11 我參加一場跨產業交流會。
I take part in a cross-industrial exchange meeting.

12 我和同儕舉辦讀書會。
I hold a study session with my peers.

13 我參加公司外部有關履約問題的研討會。
I attend a seminar on compliance outside the company.

14 我在一家電腦補習班上課，學習基礎電腦技能。
I study at a computer training school and learn basic computer skills.

15 我用功準備資格考試。
I study to prepare for a certification exam.

tips

⑪ take part in（參加）也可改用 attend。

⑭ 「我去上電腦課」可說成 I go to computer classes。

⑮ certification 是指「證明；檢定」。而「認證考試；資格考試」也可說成 certified qualification exam。

⑯ keep oneself busy 就是「讓自己很忙碌」，而 work a second job 可表達「做副業；兼差」之意。「本業」則說成 one's main

16 我兼做副業讓自己忙碌。
I keep myself busy working a second job.

17 我準備自行創業。
I prepare to set up a business of my own.

18 我積極參與義工工作。
I'm actively involved in volunteer work.

19 我和女朋友在車站見面，然後去約會。
I meet my girlfriend at the station for a date.

20 我在家放鬆一下。
I wind down at home.

occupation。
⑰ set up a business 就是「開創事業」。
⑱ be actively involved in ~ 是「積極參與～；從事～」之意。
⑳ wind down（放鬆一下）也可改用 relax。另外請注意 wind 的發音為 [waɪnd]。

1 大家都還在辦公室裡，我實在沒辦法離開。
I can't leave with everyone still in the office.

2 就在我正準備下班時，課長要求我留下來加班。
The section chief asked me to work overtime just when I was about to leave.

3 也許我該改變一下，走到下一站去搭車。
Maybe I should walk to the next station for a change.

4 我每天加班，根本無法有夜生活。
I work overtime every day and don't get to have a night life.

5 我今天真是倒楣透頂。你介意我向你抱怨一下嗎？
I had such a bad day. Do you mind if I complain to you about it?

6 一杯啤酒能讓我恢復元氣。
A beer will revitalize me.

leave = 離開;走掉(過去式和過去分詞為 left)／with ~ = 在~的狀態下／still = 依舊;還

「我 6 點下班」就說成 I leave the office at 6:00 [o'clock].。而「我提早下班」則是 I leave work early.。

---

section chief = 課長／ask ~ to ... = 要求~做…／work overtime = 加班／be about to ~ = 即將~;正要~

「我原本沒打算加班」可說成 I wasn't planning on working overtime.,而「我昨天加了兩小時的班」則說 I worked two hours overtime yesterday.。

---

walk to ~ = 走到~／next <u>station</u>/<u>stop</u> = 下一站／for a change = 和平常不同地;為了改變一下

「我為了維持健康,每天走路到車站」可說成 I walk to the station every day to keep in shape.。另,通常大站(如火車站)用 station 表示,小站(如公車站)用 stop 表示。

---

get to ~ = 得到~的機會／night life = 夜生活

此例的後半句也可說成 don't have the chance to go out at night(沒機會在晚上出去玩)。

---

such ~ = 如此的~／have a bad day = 有個倒楣的一天;一整天運氣不好／Do you mind if ~? = 你是否介意~?／complain = 抱怨;發牢騷

此例的第二句也可改成 Can I complain to you about it a little?。

---

revitalize = 使~重新恢復元氣 cf. vitalize = 賦予~活力

a beer 可指「一杯或一罐啤酒」。「工作後來上一杯啤酒特別美味!」可說成 A beer after work tastes so good!。

7　現今，新進員工似乎都不想和別人一起出去。

Nowadays, new employees don't seem to want to go out with others.

8　劉小姐其實非常健談又好相處，和她在工作時給我們的印象不同。

Unlike the image we have of her at work, Ms. Liu is very talkative and easy to get along with.

9　他一喝酒，就會說出真心話。

When he drinks, he says what he's really thinking.

10　即使喝著酒，我的腦袋依舊離不開工作。

I can't get work off my mind even though I'm having a drink.

11　好！就讓我們一路喝到天亮吧！

OK! Let's drink till dawn!

12　抱歉，我完全不會喝酒。

Sorry, but I can't drink at all.

nowadays = 現今／new employee = 新進員工／seem to ~ = 似乎~／go out with~ = 和~出去 cf. get along with ~ = 和~和睦相處／associate with ~ = 和~建立關係

「我不想為了交際應酬而去喝酒」就說成 I don't want to go drinking just to socialize.。

unlike ~ = 和~不一樣／image = 印象；形象／at work = 在工作時（也可說成 when she's working）／talkative = 健談的；愛講話的／easy to ~ = 容易~

「見過一次面後，就改變了我對她的印象」可說成 I changed my image of her after I met her once.。

what he's really thinking = 他真正的想法（what 為包含先行詞的關係代名詞，相當於 the thing(s) which）

「我把真正的感覺和公開的行為分得很清楚」可說成 I separate my real feelings and what I do in public.。而「我想知道他真正的想法」則可說成 I want to know what he is really thinking.。

get ~ off one's mind = 忘掉~／even though ~ = 即使~；儘管~／have a drink = 喝一杯

此例的前半句也可改成 I keep thinking about work「我一直想著工作」。

drink = 喝；喝酒／till dawn = 直到天亮（dawn = 黎明）

「讓我們在外面喝他個一整晚」可說成 Let's stay out and drink all night.。另外，約人喝酒時，「一起去喝一杯吧」就說成 Let's go for a drink.。

not ~ at all = 完全不~

「我不太能喝（那麼多）」則說成 I can't drink (that) much.。

13 若大家平均分攤費用，那對不喝酒的人是不公平的。
If we split the bill, then it won't be fair to those who don't drink.

14 在經理喝醉並開始說教前，讓我們先閃人吧。
Let's leave before the manager gets drunk and starts to lecture everyone.

15 你瞧已經這麼晚了！我真的必須走了。
Look at the time! I really have to go.

16 可惡！我錯過了回家的最後一班車。
Shoot! I've missed the last train home.

17 你今晚的聯誼能露一下臉嗎？我們得讓男女生人數相同才行。
Can you show up for the mixer tonight? We need to have the same number of men and women.

18 我希望能在今晚的聯誼會上遇見談得來的對象。
I hope I can meet someone I can enjoy talking to at the mixer tonight.

split the bill = 分攤費用（split = 分割；分攤）／be fair to ～ = 對～是公平的（fair = 公平的）／those who don't drink = 不喝酒的人們

「含酒精的飲料」叫 alcoholic beverages，「不含酒精的飲料」則叫 non-alcoholic beverages。

---

leave = 離開／get drunk = 喝醉／lecture = 說教；訓話

「醫生一直告誡我喝太多酒的危險」就說成 The doctor has been lecturing me on the dangers of drinking too much.。

Look at the time! = 看看時間（竟然已經這麼晚了）！／have to go = 必須要走了（也可將 go 改為 run）

「我不知道已經這麼晚了」說成 I didn't know it was this late.。

Shoot! = 糟糕！；可惡！／miss = 錯過／the last train home = 回家的最後一班列車（the last train = 末班列車）

而「我趕上了最後一班〔回家的〕列車」則說成 I caught the last train [home].。

---

show up for ～ = 在～露臉／mixer = 聯誼（也可直接用 party）／need to ～ = 必須～；需要～／the same number of ～ = 相同數量的～

「我們的男女生人數不相等」說成 We don't have the same number of men and women.。

---

meet = 遇見／enjoy talking to ～ = 享受與～談話；和～聊得開心

「我真的和你聊得很開心」說成 I really enjoyed talking with you.。而「我們之間有某些（沒有）共通點」就說成 We have <u>something</u> (<u>nothing</u>) in common.。

19 今天參加派對的人都很有氣質又長得好看。
Everyone at today's party is classy and good-looking.

20 我對他的表現印象深刻。
I'm impressed with his performance.

21 我要順道去書店一趟，看看有什麼新書。
I'll stop by the bookstore and check the new titles/books.

22 我要準時下班，因為我已預約了美甲沙龍。
I'll leave the office on time because I have a reservation at the nail salon.

23 我提早結束今天的工作去參加演唱會。
I cut my work short today to go to the concert.

24 我可能會稍微晚一點到派對。
I might be a little late for the party.

classy = 舉止得體的；有氣質的／good-looking = 好看的

good-looking 可用來形容男生，e.g. a good-looking guy（帥哥），也可用來形容女生，e.g. a good-looking girl（美女）。

---

impressed = 印象深刻的 cf. impress = 讓人留下印象／performance = 表現；表演

「我覺得反感」說成 I'm disgusted.。

---

stop by ~ = 順道去~／bookstore = 書店／the new title = 新書（title 原指「書名」，在此轉指「書」）

「我很常在書店翻閱書籍」就說成 I often browse books in the bookstore.。

---

leave the office on time = 準時下班／have a reservation = 有預約／nail salon = 美甲沙龍

此例的後半句也可說成 I have a reservation to get my nails done.（我已預約要去做指甲）。

---

cut ~ short = 將~縮短／concert = 演唱會；音樂會（現場演唱、演奏的音樂會為 live concert）

想問「我今天可以提早下班嗎？」就說成 Can I leave [the office] early today?，而「我必須提早下班」則是 I have to leave [the office] early.。

I might be ~ = 我可能會~／a little late = 稍微晚一些

「我和女朋友約了 7 點在車站前面」就說成 I'll meet my girlfriend in front of the station at 7:00.。

25 那個人就一直唱，緊抓著麥克風不放。

That guy just keeps singing and never gives up the microphone.

26 糟糕，我忘了！我今天有瑜珈課！

Oh, I forgot! I have my yoga class today!

27 由於我大部分時間都坐在桌前辦公，很少活動，所以運動起來倍覺舒暢。

I feel great when I work out, because I work mostly at my desk and hardly ever move around.

28 我應該利用下班後的時間來提升自我。

I should spend after-work hours improving myself.

29 如果我想拓展我的職業生涯，就必須取得某些資格。

I need to have qualifications of some sort if I want to advance my career.

30 隨著年紀變大，我並不常想嘗試新的東西。

As I get older, I don't often feel like trying anything new.

keep ~ing = 一直持續～／give up ~ = 放棄～／microphone = 麥克風

此例後半句也可改成「一直不肯把麥克風交給別人」never passes the microphone to anyone else。

I forgot! = 我忘了！（forgot 是 forget 的過去式）／have class = 有課

「我忘了我今天有瑜珈課！」可説成 I forgot I had my yoga class today!。

feel great = 感覺很棒／work out = 運動；健身／work at one's desk = 在桌前辦公／mostly = 主要地；大部分時間都／hardly ever ~ = 幾乎不～；很少～／move around = 活動；四處走動

work out 指「為鍛鍊身體而做運動」，e.g. I work out at the gym every day.（我每天都到健身房運動）。

spend = 花費；度過／after-work hours = 下班後的時間；／improve oneself = 改善自己

「重新磨練自己的技能」可説成 brush up one's skills，而「增進自己對～的知識」則説成 improve one's knowledge of ~。

qualification = 資格／of some sort = 某種（sort = 種類）／advance one's career = 拓展職業生涯（advance = 推進；發展）

「我有些擔心我的未來」説成 I'm sort of worried about my future.，其中的 sort of 為「有點」之意。

as ~ = 隨著～／get older = 年歲增加／don't feel like ~ = 不想～／try anything new = 嘗試任何新事物

「你何不嘗試一些新東西？」説成 Why don't you try something new?。

31 如果情況再這樣下去，我可能會失去我的工作。我需要有一些符合市場需求的技能才行。

If things go on as they are now, I might lose my job. I need to have some marketable skills.

32 和不同公司的人會面聊天，真是具有啟發性。

It's really inspiring to meet and talk with people from other companies.

33 我必須補充我的名片。

I have to restock my business cards.

34 不知今天來的那些人是哪個產業。

I wonder what industry those people who came today are from.

35 我一回家就忍不住要繼續打電動。我對電動上癮了嗎？

I have to continue my video game as soon as I get home. Am I addicted to video games?

36 我要順道去超市一趟，因為今天冷凍食品打對折。

I will stop by the supermarket because frozen food is half-price today.

if things go on as they are = 如果事情依照這個情勢繼續下去／lose one's job = 失去工作／marketable = 有銷路的；有市場需求的

marketable 原用來指商品，e.g. a marketable product（一項有銷路的產品）。

It's really ~ to ... = 做…真的是很～／inspiring = 鼓舞人心的；啟發靈感的（inspire = 激勵；鼓舞）／people from other companies = 其他公司的人們

「認識新朋友」可說成 meet someone new。

---

restock = 補充 cf. stock = 貯存；進貨／business card = 名片

「我把我的名片放進名片夾中」說成 I put my business cards into a card holder.。而「我的名片用完了」則說成 I ran out of business cards.。

I wonder ~ = 不知是～；我很好奇～／industry = 工業；產業；業界

industry 不一定要指「工業」，它可以廣泛用來指各種產業，e.g.computer industry（電腦業）、service industry（服務業）等。

---

continue = 繼續／video game = 電動；電玩（包含電視遊戲、電腦遊戲（PC game）等）／as soon as ~ = 一～就馬上／be addicted to ~ = ～成癮；沉迷於～（addict [əˋdɪkt] 使沉溺）

此例的第二句也可改為 Am I a video game addict?，其中的 addict 為名詞用法，指「成癮者」，共唸法為 [ˋædɪkt]。

---

stop by ~ = 順道去～／supermarket = 超級市場／frozen food = 冷凍食品／half-price = 半價；打對折

「特價日；特賣日」說成 <u>bargain</u>/<u>sale</u> day，而「很划算；很便宜」可說成 It's a bargain.。

37 晚餐又要在便利商店解決了！
Another dinner from the convenience store!

38 喔，不！我忘了錄那個電視節目了！
Oh, no! I forgot to have that TV program recorded!

39 我要去把我一直很想看的那部影集整部租來看！
I'm going to rent that whole drama series I've always wanted to watch!

40 我今晚必須看完那部 DVD 才行，否則就要逾期了。
I have to watch that DVD tonight or it will be overdue.

41 兼顧工作與玩樂，是我永遠的大課題。
Trying to balance out work and play is always my biggest challenge.

another = 再一；又一／dinner = 晚餐／convenience store = 便利商店

便利商店的「便當」可用 boxed meal 表示。而「我知道靠便利商店解決晚餐對身體不好」可說成 I know it's not good for me to live on those convenience store dinners.。

I forgot to ~ = 忘了做~（forgot 為 forget 的過去式）／have ~ recorded = 把~錄下來（record = 錄音；錄影）

「我讓我太太幫我把那個節目錄下來」說成 I have my wife record that program for me.。

---

rent = 租借／whole = 全部；整體／drama series = 連續劇（series = 連續；系列）／I've always wanted to ~ = 我一直很想~

「我租了新的 DVD 片子」說成 I rented a new DVD.。而「我想看的 DVD 全都被租完了」就說成 All the DVDs I wanted to see were rented out.。

---

watch DVD = 看 DVD／or ~ = 否則~／overdue = 逾期的

「支付逾期費」可說成 pay a late fee。

---

balance out = 保持平衡；兼顧／challenge = 挑戰；課題

本句的 balance out and play 可用 balance work with play 代替。

Skit  下班篇 ———————————

積極玩樂型 vs. 宅在家裡型

Woman: **Hey, how was your weekend?**

Man: **I rented a DVD on my way home and watched it on Saturday.**

W: **You have no social life❶.**

M: **What do you mean?❷**

W: **On Saturday, I went to the gym and then went bar hopping with friends.**

M: **I stopped by the bookstore and checked the new titles on Sunday.**

W: **How thrilling❸. I studied at a computer training school and did some volunteer activities.**

M: **Well, I like to relax at home.**

W: **Can I ask you out for a drink tonight? We could sing karaoke to release some stress.**

M: **Sorry, I don't drink at all.**

W: **Oh, I forgot. I have my yoga lesson tonight.**

M: **You have the gym, bars, computer school, volunteering, karaoke and yoga. I have DVDs and books. You're right. I have no social life.**

女性：嘿，你週末過得如何？

男性：我在回家的路上租了片 DVD，禮拜六就看這片DVD。

女：你沒有社交生活嘛。

男：什麼意思？

女：我週六去了健身房，然後又和朋友去逛酒吧。

男：我週日順道去了書店一趟，看看有什麼新書。

女：還真是刺激呢。我在一間電腦補習班上課，也做一些義工活動。

男：嗯，我喜歡在家放鬆。

女：我今晚可以邀請你去喝一杯嗎？我們可以唱唱卡拉 OK 紓解壓力。

男：抱歉，我滴酒不沾。

女：噢，我忘了！我今晚有瑜珈課！

男：妳有健身房、酒吧、電腦補習班、義工活動、卡拉 OK 和瑜珈。我有 DVD 和書。妳說對了，我是沒有社交生活。

【單字片語】

❶ social life：社交生活
❷ What do you mean?：你是什麼意思？
❸ thrilling：真令人興奮的；緊張刺激的

Quick Check

讓我們一起來複習本章所介紹過的句型！請依據以下中文句子的意思，完成對應的英文句子。（答案就在本頁最下方）

❶ 我喝酒以忘卻煩惱。→P262

I ( ) ( ) my troubles.

❷ 我跑步以彌補運動不足的問題。→P263

I run to ( ) ( ) ( ) not getting enough exercise.

❸ 我兼做副業讓自己忙碌。→P265

I ( ) myself ( ) working a ( ) job.

❹ 大家都還在辦公室裡，我實在沒辦法離開。→P266

I can't ( ) ( ) everyone ( ) in the office.

❺ 即使喝著酒，我的腦袋依舊離不開工作。→P268

I can't ( ) work ( ) ( ) ( ) even though I'm having a drink.

❻ 可惡！我錯過了末班車。→P270

Shootl I've ( ) ( ) ( ) ( ) home.

❼ 我提早結束今天的工作去參加演唱會。→P272

I ( ) my work ( ) today to go to the concert.

❽ 如果我想拓展我的職業生涯，就必須取得某些資格。→P274

I need to have ( ) of some sort if I want to ( )
( ) ( ).

❾ 隨著年紀變大，我並不常想嘗試新的東西。→P274

As I ( ) ( ), I don't often ( ) ( )
( ) anything new.

❿ 我一回家就忍不住要繼續打電動。我對電動上癮了嗎？→P276

I have to ( ) my video game ( ) ( ) ( ) I
get home. Am I ( ) ( ) video games?

---

❶drink/away ❷make/up/for ❸keep/busy/ second ❹leave/with/still ❺get/off/my/ mind ❻missed/the/last/train ❼cut/short

❽qualifications/advance/my/career ❾get/ older/feel/like/trying ❿continue/as/soon/as/ addicted/to

國家圖書館出版品預行編目資料

老闆要你學英文—職場句型篇 / 吉田研作, 荒井貴和, 武藤克彦　作 ;
陳亦苓翻譯. -- 初版. -- 臺北市：貝塔, 2012. 08
　　面：　公分

　ISBN: 978-957-729-894-2（平裝附光碟片）

　1. 英語　2. 會話

805.188　　　　　　　　　　　　　　　　　　101013480

老闆要你學英文—職場句型篇

作　　者／吉田研作、荒井貴和、武藤克彦
總 編 審／王復國
翻　　譯／陳亦苓
執行編輯／朱慧瑛

出　　版／貝塔出版有限公司
地　　址／100 台北市館前路 12 號 11 樓
電　　話／(02) 2314-2525
傳　　真／(02) 2312-3535
郵　　撥／19493777 貝塔出版有限公司
客服專線／(02) 2314-3535
客服信箱／btservice@betamedia.com.tw

總 經 銷／時報文化出版企業股份有限公司
地　　址／桃園縣龜山鄉萬壽路二段 351 號
電　　話／(02) 2306-6842

出版日期／2012 年 9 月初版一刷
定　　價／320 元
I S B N／978-957-729-894-2

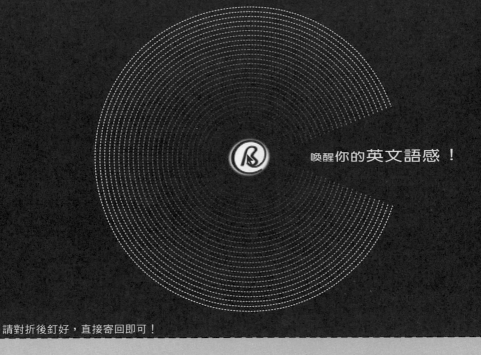

喚醒你的英文語感 ！

請對折後釘好，直接寄回即可！

100 台北市中正區館前路12號11樓

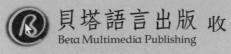 貝塔語言出版 收
Beta Multimedia Publishing

寄件者住址 □□□

貝塔語言出版
Beta Multimedia Publishing

讀者服務專線（02）2314-3535　　讀者服務傳真（02）2312-3535
客戶服務信箱　btservice@betamedia.com.tw

www.betamedia.com.tw

謝謝您購買本書！！

貝塔語言擁有最優良之英文學習書籍，為提供您最佳的英語學習資訊，您可填妥此表後寄回（免貼郵票）將可不定期收到本公司最新發行書訊及活動訊息！

姓名：＿＿＿＿＿＿＿＿＿＿　性別：☐男 ☐女 生日：＿＿＿年＿＿＿月＿＿＿日

電話：(公)＿＿＿＿＿＿＿＿＿(宅)＿＿＿＿＿＿＿＿＿(手機)＿＿＿＿＿＿＿＿＿

電子信箱：＿＿＿＿＿＿＿＿＿＿＿＿＿＿＿＿＿＿＿＿＿

學歷：☐高中職含以下 ☐專科 ☐大學 ☐研究所含以上

職業：☐金融 ☐服務 ☐傳播 ☐製造 ☐資訊 ☐軍公教 ☐出版
　　　☐自由 ☐教育 ☐學生 ☐其他

職級：☐企業負責人 ☐高階主管 ☐中階主管 ☐職員 ☐專業人士

1. 您購買的書籍是？＿＿＿＿＿＿＿＿＿＿＿＿＿＿＿

2. 您從何處得知本產品？(可複選)

　　　☐書店 ☐網路 ☐書展 ☐校園活動 ☐廣告信函 ☐他人推薦 ☐新聞報導 ☐其他

3. 您覺得本產品價格：

　　　☐偏高 ☐合理 ☐偏低

4. 請問目前您每週花了多少時間學英語？

　　　☐ 不到十分鐘 ☐ 十分鐘以上，但不到半小時 ☐ 半小時以上，但不到一小時

　　　☐ 一小時以上，但不到兩小時 ☐ 兩個小時以上 ☐ 不一定

5. 通常在選擇語言學習書時，哪些因素是您會考慮的？

　　　☐ 封面 ☐ 內容、實用性 ☐ 品牌 ☐ 媒體、朋友推薦 ☐ 價格☐ 其他＿＿＿＿＿

6. 市面上您最需要的語言書種類為？

　　　☐ 聽力 ☐ 閱讀 ☐ 文法 ☐ 口說 ☐ 寫作 ☐ 其他＿＿＿＿＿＿

7. 通常您會透過何種方式選購語言學習書籍？

　　　☐ 書店門市 ☐ 網路書店 ☐ 郵購 ☐ 直接找出版社 ☐ 學校或公司團購

　　　☐ 其他＿＿＿＿＿＿＿

8. 給我們的建議：＿＿＿＿＿＿＿＿＿＿＿＿＿＿＿＿＿

＿＿＿＿＿＿＿＿＿＿＿＿＿＿＿＿＿＿＿＿＿＿＿＿＿＿＿

學好英文 改變一生

改變一生的英文閱讀「閱」來越好！

Follow政大陳超明教授3Book曲，聽讀理解「閱」來越好！

BOOK 1
搞定「聽力」，破除學英文心理障礙！

- 8大聽力盲點各個擊破
- 嚴選11類聽力測驗必考題材
- 各種情境都能聽懂語意，溝通零失誤

定價
350元
附MP3

BOOK 2
愛上「閱讀」，聽說讀寫越來越上手！

- 獨門拆句法，化繁為簡，讀、寫雙向精通
- 大考、多益等考題為範例，各類考試飆速通關
- 母語人士泛讀的Real-Life English，
  帶你讀通實用英語各類領域素材

定價
350元

BOOK 3
「單字」輕鬆背，任何英檢考試無往不利！

- 大考單字只有1500字要背，精準、省力備考！
- 選字高明，翻譯、作文突顯個人優勢，獲致高分！
- 趨勢新字搶先收錄：3D動畫、綠能環保、
  基因工程…等時事字彙。

定價
400元
附MP3

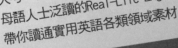

就靠英文改變你的一生！

閱讀、聽力考題破解；指考、學測衝刺；大考聽力必勝

更多詳盡書訊

貝塔語言出版
Beta Multimedia Publishing

Get a Feel for English !

喚醒你的英文語感！